A HOME FOR LOVE

by

ALY GRADY

TELEMACHUS PRESS

This book is a work of fiction. Names, characters, places and incidents are either the product of the author's imagination or are used fictitiously. Any resemblance to actual persons, living or dead, or to actual events or locales is entirely coincidental.

A HOME FOR LOVE
Copyright © 2017 ALY GRADY. All rights reserved, including the right to reproduce this book, or portions thereof, in any form. No part of this text may be reproduced, transmitted, downloaded, decompiled, reverse engineered, or stored in or introduced into any information storage and retrieval system, in any form or by any means, whether electronic or mechanical without the express written permission of the author. The scanning, uploading, and distribution of this book via the Internet or via any other means without the permission of the publisher is illegal and punishable by law. Please purchase only authorized electronic editions and do not participate in or encourage electronic piracy of copyrighted materials.

The publisher does not have any control over and does not assume any responsibility for author or third-party websites or their content.

Cover Designed by Telemachus Press, LLC

Cover Art:
Copyright © iStockphoto/172847171/twohumans
Copyright © iStockphoto/506757982/g-stockstudio

Published by Telemachus Press, LLC
www.telemachuspress.com

Visit the author web page
www.alygrady.com

Visit the author facebook page
https://www.facebook.com/AlyGrady2012

ISBN: 978-1-945330-55-1 (eBook)
ISBN: 978-1-945330-56-8 (Paperback)

FICTION / Romance / Contemporary / Design

Version 2017.04.15

10 9 8 7 6 5 4 3 2 1

For Sharon

A HOME FOR LOVE

Chapter One

STARING AT THE blueprint laying on her desk, Charlotte couldn't help her lack of concentration. The work routine of being an interior designer comforts, calms; but she lost that feeling. Helping clients achieve their dream look, feel, desire in their home usually excited Charlotte, but not today. Two days ago her personal life had fallen apart. Pulling another tissue from the box, Charlotte cleared her head right into the tissue. It was time to concentrate on work. It was work that kept her from pulling out her hair as she tried to pull herself together.

Holding the last tissue she wiped her nose and threw it in the full basket at her feet. Loud snoring from her dog Sam caught her attention, and she looks over to him sleeping on his bed. His relaxed state calmed her. "Good boy, Sam."

The phone buzzed on her desk and Jessica told her *HE* was in the lobby and wanted to see her. "Have him wait a few and then send him in." Gritting her teeth the room grew warm, a sure sign her blood pressure was on the rise.

Throbbing pain worked its way to the base of her skull, and the tension across her shoulders would take a week of massage therapy to get rid of. Charlotte was sure, if someone could see her, smoke would be seen coming out her ears. Grant had some nerve, showing up at her office, her sanctuary—to do what, gloat? He was an ass, and deep down she knew it.

It had been two days since Charlotte had been forced to move out of the home she shared with that lowlife scum. Two days of reliving the moment she walked into her home and saw him with his secretary. Two days spent alone, thinking about the shattered dreams of a life with that man and the family they wouldn't ever have. It was probably for the best; she never did stop taking the pill.

Deciding to live in a hotel, Charlotte couldn't face the disappointment from her parents. She knew her mother's questions would be never-ending, and she just didn't have it in her to answer them right now. She wasn't even sure she knew the answers to most questions involving her personal life anyhow. Her parents loved her to the point of wanting to bubble wrap her.

Thirty years old and running home to Mommy and Daddy isn't right. She loves them fiercely, but the hour-long drive to and from the office each day made it impractical, even if it would be a temporary arrangement. She is an independent person who runs her own company and makes decisions that involve thousands of dollars every day; she could make decisions on her own involving where she lived without consulting her parents. Right? She was still trying to figure out exactly where she was going to go from here, though, runny nose, puffy eyes and all. A hug from Mom right now would be nice, though.

Easing the elastic holding her hair in place, Charlotte hoped it would help the ache in her head. Kneading her scalp helped slightly. She knew her real headache was about to walk in the door. Her straight black hair fell down her back, although she usually wore it up in a ponytail. Deciding for a change to go along with the other change in her life, Charlotte used a small mirror from inside her desk to adjust her appearance. She checked her copper-colored eyes. A little mascara, a little eyeliner, and her eyes were done. She could face Grant.

At five-foot-four, she wasn't the tallest person, but she loved shoes and felt more professional, maybe even a little more powerful, in a sexy heel. She could always tell when a guy was looking at her legs, and she could get them to agree to work on anything. Sometimes, if a little eye candy was needed, she used that advantage to get what the client asked for.

Closing her eyes she breathed in through her nose and out her mouth. She allowed the comfort of her office, her haven, to calm her shaken nerves. The earth tones used to decorate the space quieted her overwrought mind. The silks on the windows were the feminine touches that reminded her of who she was, a sophisticated woman with classic taste. It was her space to work in and meet with clients, but it was also her place to go in order to step away from the crazy, testosterone-filled world of the construction industry.

Jessica knocked and stepped into her office. Sam, Charlotte's labradoodle, ran over for a pat on the head and went back to lie down on his bed in the corner. "I need to remind you about the new subcontractor, Luke Anderson. You should have checked up on him. Maybe he's called and said he received a package addressed to you? Maybe he's holding on the phone?"

"Jessica, checking out a guy is the last thing I need right now. What does he want?" An echoing clunk rung out as she dropped the empty tissue box into the trash. Charlotte opened her desk drawer and grabbed another box. Her hands slid through her hair in frustration at being forced to live in a hotel and not being able to find the exact type of residence she would like, Charlotte didn't even want to think about the male species for the foreseeable future.

Jessica looked back over her shoulder with a sheepish grin. "He said he wanted to drop off some paperwork that was brought to the job by accident. I kind of thought taking the call before seeing Grant might be a fun little payback of sorts. Just saying." She shrugged her shoulders, still smiling.

Shaking her head, Charlotte smiled at her assistant. "You make me laugh. Fine, send the call through and have Grant take a seat."

Charlotte sat back down at her desk and was looking over a contract for a new client when her desk phone rang. "Charlotte Cavanaugh."

"Miss Cavanaugh, Luke Anderson. Listen, I'm holding an envelope addressed to you. I just want to know what you want me to do with it."

"Thank you for calling. If you tell me which project you're working at I can run by."

"I'm currently at the Elmwood house."

"I'll head that way in a bit to pick it up. If you don't have any objection, that is? I'd like to do a walk-through of the house anyhow."

"*Mi Casa et tu casa*. My home is yours."

"I'll see you in a little while then."

The click of the phone echoed around the room. It reminded Charlotte she was alone once again in her office. Well, Sam was with her, even if he did sleep all the time.

Vibrations bounced her cell, alerting Charlotte of an incoming call. The tenor of Luke Anderson's voice replayed in her mind. Distracted, she answered. "Charlotte Cavanaugh, how may I help you?"

"Charlotte, dear, it's your mother."

"Oh hi, Mom, I wasn't paying attention when I answered. It's nice to hear your voice during the middle of the week. How are you and Dad?" Squeaking out her question, feeling like she was caught doing something wrong, Charlotte sat back in her chair with her head hanging down.

"We're fine. You sound stuffy. Make sure to take your vitamins. Listen, I wanted to invite you and Grant over for dinner if you don't already have plans this weekend."

"Hmm, that's probably a very good idea. I have a few things to talk with you about, too. Grant won't be able to make it, though."

"We could wait and have both of you over another time."

"No, I'll come. Let me see how the rest of my week goes. Is that all right? I have a few things in the works that might make my weekend crazy."

"That's fine. Let me know which day works best for you."

"Thanks, Mom. Love you. I'll call soon." She hung up and wondered if the large envelope Luke Anderson had was the fabric samples she had requested for the Sullivan's house. *The Sullivan's ... Grant was their general contractor ... and he was still sitting in her lobby ... oh well, waiting a little might do him some good.*

Charlotte picked up her office phone. "Jessica, can you tell Grant I can see him now? I got a little sidetracked." There was nothing she could do about her puffy eyes. Maybe seeing her would make Grant feel badly for being a cheating bastard.

He entered the room and the dog didn't even look up. Charlotte slid back in her executive chair, placing her fingers under her chin. She had several client meetings that day and was in a fabulous blouse that brought attention to her face. When she dressed that morning she thought that maybe if she looked good she would feel good. It had worked for a while.

Grant had always said that he had been attracted to her professional presence. Maybe she should find someone who appreciated her for herself and not just her business acumen. She'd work on that.

"What can I do for you, Grant? I'm pretty sure I have all my personal belongings out of our ... your house."

"Charlotte." He started to walk forward.

Raising her hands, palms facing out, stopped Grant in his tracks. Tightness spread across the muscles of her shoulders. Her jaw clamped shut, clinching her teeth. Turning her head she focused on her sleeping dog. Anger and sadness churned inside her aching heart.

"Charlotte, I think we should talk." His softly worded statement sounded sincere, but it was spoken too late.

"Grant, the time for talking is long gone," she spoke through clinched teeth. Charlotte took a deep breath and relaxed her mouth in an effort to keep her composure. "You lost that opportunity when you decided to take your secretary to our house and bang her on the washing machine. Crap, Grant, that is so cliché." She stood up and slid her hands down to smooth her pencil skirt, then placed her hands on her hips. He stepped back at her commanding presence. The four-inch heels helped bring her up to his level. Looking at this sap standing in front of her, she realized that while she was upset about how things had unfolded, she wasn't upset about the loss of the relationship. However, having to move out of the house she'd devoted herself to designing and making it their home was a crushing blow.

"We should go out."

"Stop talking right now. You'll embarrass yourself. The best thing that happened to me was walking in on you the other day. It's opened my eyes to what our relationship was really based on: professional mutual respect. You're great at your job. The detail you go into with every project we have worked on together is exacting. I think you feel the same way. Let's face it, if you respected me as much in our relationship, you wouldn't have felt compelled to stray."

Sitting down heavily in one of the client chairs Grant focused his attention at his feet. "So, you're saying we shouldn't try to stay together?"

Charlotte sat down as well, and folded her hands on top of her desk. "We are in no way going to try to stay together." The tension that only moments earlier weighed her down lessened. Realizing that her life was moving forward without him was exactly what she wanted to happen.

"Are you still going to work on the Sullivan, Camden and Gamboni projects?"

"Yes. My firm has already invested considerable time in those three projects. As a business decision, it's a good idea to keep them alive. But I want you to know that in the future, I won't necessarily be able to drop other things just for your clients. You lost the opportunity to get to the front of the line."

He stood up. "I understand, and thank you for keeping those three clients. You're right, my dear, we do work well together." He turned and started to walk toward the door. Reaching for the door handle he paused and looked back. "We were good together once, weren't we? You did mean something more than a business contact with benefits. I think we both thought it was more."

Charlotte closed her eyes to ward off the hurt that ending their relationship caused her. Looking once more, directly, she peered into his brown eyes with resolve to move forward with her life. "I did think it was good. That was up till the moment you tossed it on the floor and stomped on it. There is no going back, Grant. Let's move forward with our businesses and leave it at that."

He let out a long breath. "I get it." He turned back to the door and left the office, closing the door with a soft click behind him.

Thudding against the office door, Charlotte's shoe landed silently on the carpeted floor. Flopping back into her chair just as Jessica walked in, she blew out her breath.

Jessica looked over her shoulder before looking back at her boss and friend. "So, what did the jerk have to say?"

"It's so good to have you in my corner." Charlotte smiled. She sat forward and ran her hands over the gathering at the shoulder seams of her blouse. "I think what it comes down to is that he's covering his hide. We have those three clients of his he didn't want to lose face with."

Jessica retrieved the thrown shoe and handed it over. "No, 'I'm sorry and I want you back'?" Folding her arms across her chest, she showed her own anger toward Grant.

"Oh, he tried at first with 'we should go out.' When I shot him down he changed his tune. He screwed up, getting caught, but we all know it wasn't going to work out in the end. I figured out only just today that I didn't love him. I loved the idea of him and me together. How together we made a great couple. He's the general contractor and me the designer. Blah blah blah … I could romanticize it all I wanted, but he just wasn't the guy for me." Blinking quickly, Charlotte held her threatening tears at bay.

Charlotte watched Jessica wrinkle her nose. "So, you're saying he really only came here to cover his butt? He's so slimy."

"He is what he is. I know my calendar is full. Do you have anything new for me?" Grant was already moving into her past, and she was moving into her future.

"While you were talking with Grant, a call came in from Mr. Brentwood. We worked with him and his wife on their vacation home on the shore and then their cabin in New Hampshire. It sounds as though Mrs. Brentwood now wants to make some changes to their house in Easthampton."

"Forward me their contact information and I'll set that up. Let me make a call to the Harrisons." Lifting the cellphone to start back to work she pointed it toward Jessica. "One more thing. I need you to set up installation with the Wilsons."

"Sure thing." Jessica headed toward the door and turned. "I almost forgot. Your mother called."

"I talked to her before I saw Grant. She wants to have dinner with me and, of course, Grant. I know she loves me, but trying to be a perfect daughter is sometimes too much to handle." She shook her head. "I need to focus on things for today."

"I hear you. Parents, you've gotta love them, though." Jessica left and Charlotte sat back in her chair. Shaking her head again, she laughed at how the day was unfolding. She still didn't have a place to live, but she felt better about moving forward. If closure was what had just happened with Grant, then it did help. Looking down at the note she made for herself she smiled. Focus on work. Life moves forward.

Charlotte finished organizing her files. Packing up necessary samples and notes along with her laptop, she walked down the hall toward the reception "Jessica, I'm heading out. I need to bring Sam back to his doggie hotel, and then I'm stopping to check a few things. Call me if you need anything."

Design files lay spread across her desk as Jessica worked to organize them the way Charlotte expected. Waving toward her boss, she acknowledged Charlotte's departure. "I will. See you later."

Chapter Two

"DUDE, YOU'VE ONLY been back from your mother's funeral in Georgia a few days. You should take some more time for yourself."

He knew he was being rude, but Luke couldn't help it. Standing at the work bench with his back to his best friend, Joe, he closed his eyes to shut out the memory of his loss. Even the mention of his beloved mother's death forced a lump in his throat that never seemed to want to clear. Luke stroked the stubble of his beard, reminding himself just how little time he took for himself. "I'm fine. There was nothing left for me to do, so I came back. Sitting in my house doesn't make sense either."

"I get that. Well, if down the line you need to take time off, just do it."

"Thanks. I still have a few things here I need to settle with my mom's property. She made me promise to sell it to someone that would have a family if I wasn't going to have one of my own."

Turning now to face Joe, he saw the way he stroked his chin. "You do know that you can just tell the realtor to sell that property?"

Joe stopped stroking his chin and Luke picked up a hammer. Walking over to the shelf he was constructing, Luke placed the board where he needed it. "I can't have the realtor sell it to just anyone. I made a promise it would be sold to the right person. I can't go back on that. It's the last thing we talked about before she slipped into unconsciousness. She never woke up again."

That last thought made it hard to breathe. Tears formed and he swallowed to hold his emotions at bay. The hammer in his hand weighed thirty pounds and he took all his anger out on the nail head. Cancer didn't discriminate and in his mom's case, it sure moved swiftly.

***

Step number one in moving forward was finding Mr. Luke Anderson. The envelope that he contacted her about contained fabric samples. Moving forward with her upside down life would be the new plan. Focusing, Charlotte decided, was her new goal; and achieving it started with getting the fabric samples.

Charlotte approached the door and realized that knocking on it would prove futile. The door didn't exist. Pounding hammers and the whine from the blade of a saw masked any effort Charlotte made to inform the construction crew of her arrival.

Gruff, clipped instructions from the gentleman crouched in the corner facing the wall proved the only sign of life after the entryway.

"Wait, wait you stupid idiot." Turning only his head he yelled over his shoulder. "You by the door, what do you want?"

Charm was certainly lacking, but she was only looking for her envelope. "I was told I'd find Luke Anderson here."

"Figures. He's in the back of the house." He turned back toward the wall, back to work. "Can you please grab the damn wire I'm feeding ya?!"

"Thank you." Knowing full well the guy was no longer paying attention to her, politeness won out.

Taking stock of the interior detail of this house, Charlotte was jealous she wasn't in charge of decorating it. Walking past the sweeping staircase and down the short hall she entered a sitting area. The brand new construction replicated details from a past generation.

Running a successful interior design firm required organization and trustworthy people, as well as a list of trusted tradesmen she could call on. For the bigger projects she took on, she had brought Grant in as the general contractor, and he handled the coordination of the different subcontractors. Skimming her fingers along the fireplace mantle, she appreciated the craftsmanship in front of her. It wasn't like anything Grant had ever asked for. This construction site, Charlotte quickly estimated, would be a five thousand square feet home. This would be a house she would have gotten a general contractor for.

Thumping of construction boots alerted Charlotte to an approaching worker. "Can I help you?"

"Sorry, I was just studying the detail around the fireplace."

"It is nice, isn't it? Are you the homeowner?"

"Oh, no, I'm sorry. I'm Charlotte Cavanaugh, Interior Designer." Extending her hand she grasped his dust covered hand.

"You will have a fun time filling this monster with furniture."

"Oh, I'm not. This project isn't mine. I'm just here to pick something up from Luke Anderson."

"Huh, he was right behind me a second ago. Follow me, maybe he went back to the study."

***

He stepped back to inspect the last board he nailed in place. Even if he did pat himself on the back, Luke was proud of the job he did. So wrapped up on his own work, he barely heard one of his workmen on the first floor yell up that a lady was at the front of the house staring at the front door.

A woman was wandering around his job. At least the chick appreciated a quality job.

Dust motes floated around the tips of the ears of a tiger cat, which had slipped in unnoticed. The sneaky feline crept along the base board venturing from room to room. Luke spotted the creature snaking its way past the miter saw he had stopped using moments earlier. Rubbing its head on the leg of his jeans, Luke scooped up the fur ball. "Gotcha."

"You got what?"

"This cat." He tucked the kitten in the crook of his arm. Turning, he watched the sunlight dance off the top of her head. She stood just inside the doorway smiling at him. The need to explain his actions tumbled from his lips. "She, or is it a he?" Lifting the intruder, he inspected the furry underside. "She has been in and out of the house for days. The guys think it's cute we have a job site pet. She could get hurt being in here, so I need to bring her to a rescue."

"A rescue is a great option. At least she'll have a fighting chance at finding a good home." Closing her lips brought his attention to her jaw. Traveling past her jaw, Luke continued to survey her neck. She cleared her throat and he watched the tendons tense and relax. She did it again and it dawned on him he had been caught staring at her.

"Sorry. It's been a long day."

"You called my office earlier. I'm Charlotte Cavanaugh." Long, slender fingers extended toward him.

Wrapping his work roughened hands around smooth, soft hands distracted him. Startled, Luke suddenly realized he wasn't acting professional at all. Letting go, he immediately felt the loss of her warm hands. "Yes, I did call." He cleared his throat. "I have a rather large envelope that was delivered here, but addressed to you. I thought you would want whatever was inside. Follow me." He secured the cat in his arm and motioned with his free hand.

Clicking of her heals on the wooden floor allowed Luke's thoughts to wander to visions of gliding his fingertips up the curve of her calf. Slender, toned legs. He would admit it any day; he was a leg man.

"I kept the package here since I knew you were going to pick it up today." Luke lifted the large envelope from the counter in the kitchen. His fingertips touched hers. He had to smile at the goofy thought of sparks flying in the air like from an old school romance story. Looking at her eyes and the small smile on her lush lips he thought she might be thinking the same thing.

"I guess that is it then. Thank you." She raised the envelope slightly, but didn't make eye contact.

He thought she might have blushed.

"Come on, I'll walk you out so you don't get attacked by rabid kittens." Luke held up the kitten he still had cradled in his left arm.

Passing the fireplace Charlotte paused. "This is a wonderful surround. Traditional. Did someone do all the inlay by hand?" Her fingers ran along the top board. Caressing.

"Yes," he cleared his throat to start again. "Yes, I did." *Damn it.* Heat worked its way up his body. He knew he was turning red. He never blushed at a compliment to his work. Why start now?

"It's very nice." She looked over his shoulder. "I shouldn't take any more of your time. Thank you again for notifying me you had this."

Walking her to the front hall he said his goodbye. The walk back to his work bench felt like he had cement in his shoes. What he really wanted to be doing was chatting some more with the attractive interior designer. Thoughts of Charlotte were the first bright spot to happen for Luke in a long time.

"Someone find the intern. I need to get this cat out of here so I can work."

***

Driving away from Luke Anderson created an interesting curiosity for Charlotte. Emotions still ran razor quick and she attributed the pull to the attractive carpenter as just that, curiosity. Other fish in the sea and all that.

Work was her grounding factor, and she was going to focus on that. Being in charge suited her perfectly. Designwise, she was precise, and on a jobsite she was quick to make decisions on the fly to keep the project moving yet still keep her designs.

Like the Brentwood's, the couple Charlotte had spoken with earlier, she had many repeat clients. Some started off with her changing over a simple powder room, so they could see her design style and work ethic, and then they moved on to bigger projects. Others called her after seeing the work she had done for someone else. In the beginning, Charlotte had worked on a few show houses for charity events to help promote herself and her new design business. She still did show houses, but now she was able to enlist the help of her entire staff to get the work done. Having a staff to call on was the benefit of several years of hard work, which she had done completely on her own.

Running around to check on construction progress for a few clients, Charlotte had only made a quick run through Dunkin' Donuts for a coffee earlier in the day. Now though, the late afternoon sun hung low in the sky skimming under the sun visor. Concentrating on the drive brought on Charlotte's hyperawareness of the rumble in her stomach. She was starved. Food would have to wait for one more stop. Charlotte needed to pick up several files from her desk before the meetings scheduled for the morning.

Lights were still on in the lobby, but she knew Jessica was gone, since her car wasn't in the parking lot. Unlocking the door, Charlotte saw her best friend Aimee sitting on a loveseat, looking at Architectural Digest magazine.

"Well, fancy seeing you here. This is a nice surprise. What's up?"

"It's an amazing coincidence. Jessica was about to leave when I arrived and let me in to wait for you to come back." Aimee stood, smiling, and gave Charlotte a hug. "I thought I'd see if you wanted to grab a bite to eat. The Italian place that just opened is supposed to be great."

"I'm game. Give me a second to drop off these files and get the stuff I need for the morning."

The events of the day distracted Charlotte on the drive to the restaurant, but not enough. The parking lot was packed and she still managed to see Grant's car on the other side of the lot. She got out and headed over to Aimee. "I think we need to change the venue. I'm not entirely up for Italian."

Aimee still had her door open. She looked at Charlotte and winked. The scrutiny was making Charlotte antsy. Looking over her shoulder, then back to Aimee, Charlotte shifted her weight from one foot to the other. Then Aimee tilted her head in the direction of the offending car. "Follow me. I know a burger joint down the road that Grant would never set foot in."

Chapter Three

CHARLOTTE SHOULD HAVE guessed that Aimee had heard the news of her breakup with Grant. In the tight-knit New England town, news traveled fast from neighbors taking walks and catching up in coffee shops. Not much stayed a secret, especially during the summer months.

The burger joint, as Aimee called it, was a dive bar with at least a dozen motorcycles lined up out front. Neon signs advertised a variety of adult beverages in the windows of the dark wooden building. "My brother's tending bar tonight, and no one will bother us." All eyes turned to look their way as soon as they walked in. Out of place in her skirt and heels, alongside Aimee in her black suit and white silk blouse, Charlotte wished she had on something less attention grabbing. A t-shirt and jeans perhaps? Aimee waved to the crowd and proceeded toward a booth off to the side, away from peering eyes.

Tapping from her high heels on the wooden floor rang out like firecrackers on the fourth of July. She followed

Aimee and was grateful that the floors weren't slick. A quick image came to mind of landing on her bottom in front of the room of full strangers. She pursed her lips and swallowed hard concentrating with every step. "Well Aimee, I agree, this is the last place I can see Grant coming for a drink."

"That was the idea behind coming here." Both women laughed and took a seat.

Charlotte's eyes widened. She couldn't help but stare, surprised, as a grizzly of a man walked over with two menus. "How's it going, sis?" He looked at Charlotte, who was looking back and forth between clean-cut, corporate attorney Aimee and this bear of a guy.

Recognition finally came. "It's been a long time. You're Jimmy, right? I'm Charlotte. Aimee and I were in school together. I forgot Aimee told me you owned your own business. She forgot to mention what kind of place." Turning her head she squinted at her friend then turned back to Jimmy. "You're a little older, so you probably don't remember me. I guess we both looked a lot different."

"It's just Jim these days. Nice to see you. It's been a while for sure. You haven't changed one bit." His eyes scanned Charlotte's face. "I know its past Aimee's feedbag time, so let me get you some drinks while you think about what you want."

"Just get us two lights and put on a couple burgers and fries. We're celebrating Charlotte's independence."

"Well, I'll get right on that. I'm honored you decided to do your celebrating at my humble establishment." Jim walked away with a wink and a smile in Charlotte's direction.

Charlotte looked around at all the posters and neon signs. "Your brother sure looks a lot different than he did in high school. This place is interesting. I'd never have come in here alone, but I'm glad you suggested it tonight. I like that we can sit here and be ... I don't know ... left alone."

"I've come in here a few times." Aimee smiled as she looked around the room. "I've come in here when I knew Jim was working. You're right, though, it is a great place to relax and talk. It never gets too loud, at least it hasn't when I've been here."

Jim brought back their beers and smiled at Charlotte again. He turned and walked back to the bar area.

"I think either my brother has a facial twitch, or he's smitten." Aimee took a long pull on her beer. "So, as you already guessed, Jessica called to fill me in on how things have been going for you."

Charlotte's eyebrows squished together. Catching her face in her hands, she planted her elbows on the table. She could feel the tension pull on her shoulders. Being a burden to anyone, even a friendly concern, grated on her independent spirit.

Aimee pulled her hands away. "I know that Jess shouldn't have said anything, but she worries about you, so don't be upset with her."

Charlotte blew out a huge breath and puffed up her bangs releasing the stress she had carried all day. Leaning forward, again placing her elbows on the table she contemplated her life. "I'm not mad at Jessica. I'm just pissed off at myself for even staying with Grant for as long as I did. I loved that house. I loved all the work I had put into it. I've had time to think about what Grant and I were to each other, and I realize now we weren't a good couple. He liked being able to say I was a designer and that he brought those designs to life." Charlotte paused as Jim brought over their burgers and set them on the table.

The burger, fries and beer were not a typical meal for Charlotte, and she decided she was going to enjoy every last crumb on her plate. She popped a fry into her mouth.

"Jess also told me you've been living at the Hilton for the past two nights, and Sam had to be put in a kennel. I want you to move in with me until you decide what you want to do."

Charlotte was mid sip and almost spit out her beer. She placed the beer glass on the table. "You want me to move in? Aim, while you are one of my dearest friends, we are not compatible as roommates. I'm borderline OCD, and your organizational skills are in complete contrast with mine. I'd drive you insane in a day."

"I don't like the thought of you being homeless." Aimee placed her hand on top of Charlotte's.

"Oh, my gosh, don't look at me with those puppy dog eyes. Okay, saying it like that sounds pathetic. I'm not moving in with you. Grant is scum and I'll miss living in the house, but I'll be fine. I am fine. I contacted a realtor I know, and I've had her start a search for a place. It won't be long, and if it turns out to be longer than expected, I'll suck it up and tell my parents."

Aimee gasped. "You haven't told your parents? What if there's an emergency?"

Charlotte laughed. "My parents would call my cellphone no matter what the situation was. It'll be okay. I'm having dinner with them sometime soon, and I'll tell them then. They have all these expectations. I'll fill them in on everything that happened. You know how they were hoping for me to get married. Heck, at this point I think just saying they were going to be grandparents would have been enough. They're feeling left out of their social circles not having a picture brag book."

Aimee's cell buzzed on the table and she answered, so Charlotte took a few moments to look around the bar. In the dimly lit back corner were a few tables taken up by bearded guys with lots of black leather and what appeared to be a logo on all the backs of their jackets. Only two guys were sitting at the bar. One was talking to Jim. He had brown wavy hair and a tan t-shirt stretched across broad shoulders. He looked … familiar. If he would just turn so she could see his face, maybe she could figure out where she knew him from.

Aimee ended her call. Charlotte's gaze held on the attractive man at the bar. Aimee cleared her throat. "That's Luke. He's in construction. I'm surprised you haven't run across him yet. His guys are great, friendly people. His claim to fame is the detailed finish work he does. One of my clients was divorcing and fighting to keep the house, and she went on and on about the great work he did. Now that I see him, maybe she was only impressed with the construction crew. I'd want to stay home and watch them work on my place, too."

Charlotte looked back at her friend and could feel the flush working its way up her neck. "It's Luke Anderson? I um, I already met him. Today, actually."

"You know Char, he would make an excellent rebound hook-up."

She couldn't help laughing. "I don't think so. One night stand isn't my thing." Checking out the view at the bar made her smile wider. "Mr. Anderson is pretty hot. He could make a girl think about a one night stand, though."

**

The mirror across from him allowed Luke to observe his surroundings without turning. He noticed the two women in the booth across the room and recognized one as the interior designer he met earlier in the day. Charlotte, her name is Charlotte. A classic beauty that caused his heart to skip a beat. Now, they were looking at him and it made him a little self-conscious. "Hey Jim, I'll have another beer. So what's up with the decorator and the girl scout over in the booth?"

Jimmy tilted his head toward the women. "The one in the suit is my sister, Aimee, lawyer type. You met her a while back. The other is her friend, Charlotte."

Luke glanced at them again. They were out of place by the way they were dressed. Well, when he thought about it, they were out of place simply for being female. Luke knew most of the guys in the place, and a few brought their wives to the bar, but not very often. It was kind of nice to look over and see some eye candy.

"Let's send them over something sweet for dessert." Luke thought for a second. "I had one of these at that all-inclusive I was working on last summer. It's called the Girl Scout. A shot." Scrolling on his phone he searched for the recipe.

Jim rolled his eyes. "Okay, what's in it?"

"Found it. It's a half-ounce Bailey's, half-ounce Kahlua, and the one I had was half-ounce crème de menthe, but I think it's really supposed to be peppermint schnapps."

"Shit man, that's girly." Jim went about making the drink, shaking his head. He poured the mixture into large shot glasses and walked them over to his sister's table. Speaking loud enough for Luke to overhear Jim placed the shot glasses on the table. "The guy at the bar bought these for you. I'd say it's a perfect drink for you girls."

Charlotte took her shot glass and gave Luke a salute. "So what's in it?" She practically yelled it so Luke could hear. She smelled the tiny glass.

"Try it and if you like it, what's in it don't matter."

The girls raised the glasses to each other and sipped. Jim walked back to the bar with a huge smile on his face. "Now you started it. The girls bought you a beer and want to share their cookie shot. They're buying the next round."

Luke declined the shot, since he was driving. Squeaking from the front door alerted everyone in the bar to new arrivals. A few people left. The entire time he was there, Luke kept an eye on the booth in the corner. Laughter and a few high pitched squeals invaded that area of the testosterone filled bar. The women seemed to be having a good time. Every once in a while they would wave at him when Jim went over to see if they needed anything.

At eleven, Jim flashed the lights, signaling last call. That was when the women gathered their belongings and, laughing, made their way over to the bar.

"Brother dear, I can't believe you're closing so early. It's like nine o'clock."

Jim cupped Aimee's chin with his enormous hand. "It's a school night. Okay, so you're a big girl now, but you two've been over there laughing and carrying on all night. You were here even longer than the regulars." He waved his other hand around to indicate the now empty space.

Charlotte and Aimee laughed again. "Oops. We were just having fun chatting about old times." Charlotte stuck out her hand toward Luke. "Thank you for the yummy after dinner drink. We took our time with it, but it was a good one."

Luke took her hand and held it. Looking down, he couldn't help himself with a quick peek at how she looked. But it was the feel of her skin next to his that held his attention. Long fingers wrapped around his work rough hands. The contrast with her softer, gentler hand couldn't be missed. She hadn't changed from when he saw her earlier. Obviously, she hadn't planned to be in a biker bar. Around her neck she wore a necklace with green and gold baubles. Her mouth smiling and her eyes twinkling with unknown mischief. He smiled back. "It was fun spending the evening with you. Next time we could even talk."

Aimee kissed her brother on the cheek. "Looks like we should head home."

Jim grabbed his sister's keys. "Oh no you don't. You'll be getting door to door service tonight." Jim groaned. "I have my bike tonight. I need to drive your car, little sis."

Luke looked at Charlotte. "Do you have your own car here? I don't mind bringing you to where you need to go."

The women laughed. "I do," Charlotte said. "But I can drive, really, I'm fine. I don't want to be a bother."

"It's no bother. No need to take chances. Jim, you take your sis and I'll bring Miss Charlotte home. Since I'm responsible for sending drinks your way, I can at least help with driving."

"Um …" Charlotte hesitated and looked to her friend.

Aimee placed her hand on Charlotte's arm. "Thank you, Luke. Remember, my brother knows where you live, so you better be on your best behavior."

"Yes, ma'am." Aimee kissed him on the cheek and Luke placed his hand on the small of Charlotte's back as they walked toward the only truck in the parking lot. "I'll have to lift you up into the seat." Charlotte just nodded turning to face him. He put his hands around her tiny waist. "Up you go." Lifting her up into the passenger seat of his truck, he caught the scent of her sweet perfume. He stepped up on the runner so he could put her seatbelt on. As he reached across her to click it in place, he was face to face with her.

Her eyes pulled him in, and he moved the slightest bit closer.

Charlotte moved closer too, leaning in to nuzzle his neck. "You're very handsome. You do know that, right? That southern accent is really sexy. I can't imagine you don't have a girlfriend?"

"Miss Charlotte, I think you might make it hard for a guy to be gentlemanly. No, I don't have a girlfriend. It's a good thing I know Jim will kick my ass if I don't toe the line. I'm going to shut this door and get in on my side of the truck." He did just that, jumping up into the driver seat of his F-250 crew cab truck. "Where to, my lady?"

Charlotte turned in her seat, running her hand along the leather armrest. "Would it sound too weird if I said I'm currently living at the Hilton on Main Street?" She looked down into her lap.

"I'd think it was a come-on, except you're a little uncomfortable even telling me. I'm sure there's a story to this one, but we can leave that for another time."

Luke pulled out of the parking lot and headed toward the hotel Charlotte was currently calling home. Driving his truck up to the circular drive in front of the hotel he shifted the truck into park. "Wait a second. I'll help get you out."

Jumping out, Luke ran his finger along the chrome detail on the hood of his truck. The idea of bringing Charlotte home surprised him. Now that he arrived he wasn't sure how to proceed. This wasn't a date. They hadn't even spent any real time getting to know one another. Getting to know Charlotte Cavanaugh better seemed like a really good idea, though. Snapping the door handle open, she turned to face him. Luke found himself standing in front of her with her legs against his chest. "Don't jump down. Let me help you, or you'll break a leg on those stilts you call shoes."

He eased her down, and again found himself face to face with the black-haired beauty. "Charlotte, not to sound forward, but my momma raised a gentleman, and I can't in good conscience drop you off like this. Would it be all right if I walked you to your door?"

She held up a plastic card. "My room key. I'm on the fifth floor."

Luke took the card and all sorts of thoughts ran through his mind, some not on the most honorable side. In the end, though, his momma had raised him right.

The short ride up to the fifth floor was an act of torture of the sweetest sense. Heat from her body warmed his hand, which he held at her lower back. No, he knew she didn't need him to support her. He kept his hand there to enjoy the warmth from her body. The elevator indicated the floor with a ding, and Charlotte stepped back startled. Luke's hand held her steady. "After you, my lady."

They stepped off the elevator and he held Charlotte's hand as they made their way to her hotel room door. Sliding the card through the lock he opened the door. "Good night, Miss Charlotte. I'm glad I was able to be part of your evening. You have a nice smile. I'm glad I got to see it."

Charlotte gave her head a small shake and smiled. "Thank you. It was fun to get out tonight and be around people who are … nice."

Being around a beautiful new woman without expectations for anything more, anything physical, was exciting. "I was glad I was around." He laughed at repeating himself.

"Thank you, Luke." She looked at his feet. "I'm curious. Do you always wear construction boots?" She looked up.

Luke smiled. He was surprised by the question. He scratched his day old beard. "I guess I usually do."

She stepped into her hotel room just enough to hold open the door. "Just to let you know, Aimee and I weren't drunk. We sipped that one shot all night long and drank lots of water. It's just, well, it was good of you to offer to drive me here, to make sure I was safe. Aimee said you were a good guy. Until tonight, I was pretty sure all guys were jerks. I'm glad you proved me wrong."

"Sounds like another story. We'll have to get together so I can find out about these stories." Stepping back from the doorway, Luke raised his hand in a silent goodbye.

Charlotte stepped further into her room and smiled back. "Maybe we will." She closed the door. Maybe she could move that imaginary line a little.

Chapter Four

MORNINGS SUCK. WAKING in a hotel day after day didn't make things better. Waking and realizing that your car is still in a parking lot across town slowed a sucky morning down even more. Only bright spot to a sucky morning: the sexy dream about a southern gentleman with big brown eyes and a dimple in his cheek, which tempted to be explored further. Thoughts of Luke with the dirt and dust on his work boots stopped Charlotte in her tracks. He worked hard and got dirty and wore the proof on his feet. He didn't sit around pushing a pencil or trying to sweet talk anyone. He was the real deal.

Lying in bed with thoughts of Luke brought on a nervous excitement Charlotte hadn't felt in a very long time. Butterflies raced all over her jumpy stomach just thinking back on the evening before. She enjoyed the memory so much that the reminder from her phone surprised her; she was running behind schedule. Starbucks on the way to the office was out of the question, too, because she was in a cab—her car still at the bar. The thought of going out of her way to get it made her day feel much longer. Finally, walking through the office door, Charlotte was greeted by Jessica and Aimee, full of smiles.

Standing, Aimee handed Charlotte a caramel macchiato. "I thought you might like this."

"Thanks. I'll be right back." Sipping the hot beverage, Charlotte walked down the carpeted hallway to her private office. She set her bags and jacket on her desk and walked back to the conference room. Aimee and Jess sat on the couch. "I should have a headache, but we didn't drink that much. I do have body aches, though. I think we did too much laughing, Aims."

Aimee and Jessica sat on either end of the couch. Charlotte sat between them. They leaned forward and looked at each other. Aimee looked at Jessica and then at Charlotte. "Luke Anderson drives you home after a night at a bar, and you're sitting there complaining about body aches from laughing?"

Charlotte looked from Aimee to Jess. "Oh gosh! You can't possibly think we …" She moved her hands around in the air in indignation. "Luke's a very nice guy. We chatted on the drive to the hotel, and he walked me to my room. We said goodnight. End of story. Remember, I don't do one night stands!" She got off the couch and began walking away.

Jess stood. "Listen, Charlotte, we weren't very tactful just now. Aimee and I would just love for you to find something new. You know, a fling before the next serious relationship. I can only imagine what he looks like from that sexy voice of his. He sounds hot with a capital H. A fling

with him wouldn't be something to crawl in a hole about."
The phone rang at the reception desk in the outer office.
"I'll get that."

"This is why I hate being single. Every guy I talk to,
people will assume I'm having sex with him." Charlotte
walked back to the couch and flopped down. "I haven't slept
well in days and my back is stiff. I feel icky, so thanks for the
coffee. I need it today. I have two appointments, and I still
need to get my car. The files are in it."

Aimee stood and held out her hand to help Charlotte up.
"I'll take you to your car. I have something I want to share
with you."

At a stoplight across the street from the bar where
Charlotte's car was parked, she noticed a diamond ring on
Aimee's left hand; her fourth finger sparkled. "Oh my God, is
that what I think it is on your hand?" Charlotte covered her
mouth as if a very big secret had just slipped out.

"Shush, I need to get into the parking lot before I do the
freak out with you."

Charlotte turned, a huge smile on her face. She sat patiently for the next few minutes while Aimee waited for the
traffic light to change, drove into the parking lot and found a
place to stop.

Aimee didn't even turn in her seat. She let out a screech
that made the couple walking on the sidewalk stop and look.
Charlotte waved them on.

"Can you believe it?" Aimee said. "Derek came back
from his business trip last night. He wasn't supposed to be
home till this afternoon. He was waiting and saw Jimmy
driving me home. We snuggled on the couch until we went to

bed, so sweet. When I woke up this morning, he had a tray with breakfast treats on it for me."

"Awe."

"Hush, let me finish. The coffee mug was turned over on the saucer. When I lifted it up, the ring was there, and Derek was on one knee asking me to marry him."

"Ooohhh. So sweet." Charlotte leaned over and hugged her friend. "I can't believe you didn't blurt it out before."

"Char, I wanted you to be the first to know. I realize I shouldn't be bragging about my happiness right now to you, but you're my best friend, and I couldn't imagine telling anyone else first."

"Ooohhh. More sweetness." Charlotte cleared her throat, smiling the whole time. "I think you're gonna make me cry. This almost makes up for the fact that I didn't get lucky with a really hot guy last night." They both laughed. "Not that I wanted to, but Luke Anderson is very good looking."

Aimee clapped her hands. "Sister, that man is a sight to behold. I'm glad you took notice. Now I think you should act on that."

"Aimee, I'm working on me right now, which leaves no room for a guy. Plus, work is busy and what guy would want to be second fiddle to a job. No, I'm pretty sure I'm just flying solo till I get a place to at least call home for a little while."

"Whatever you say, Charlotte. But let me say that Mr. Right will be okay waiting till you sort your shit out as long as he knows you want him to be there when everything is all said and done."

"You're probably right, but I just don't think I've found that person yet."

She and Aimee sat in the car and talked for over an hour, before realizing they both had meetings to get to.

The canopy of tree limbs shaded the road as Charlotte drove her Mercedes along Route 20 toward her client's country home. She thought about everything that had been happening in her life. Aimee's life was in fast-forward with her new engagement to Derek and the life they were building together. That made her happy, but also made her aware that her own life was at a complete standstill, possibly moving backwards. If she got desperate, she knew she could always move back in with her parents. But, she ran her own success-ful business, and there was no reason to run home to live with her parents just because a relationship hadn't worked out. She used the voice command in her car to call her realtor and modify the search parameters for a place to live.

***

From April to October, Mr. and Mrs. Charles Brentwood lived on a tree-lined lane off a winding country road in their Western Massachusetts town of Easthampton. They flew south with the rest of the northern snowbirds to their home in Palm Coast, Florida, as the weather turned chilly. Their grown children had scattered all over the country, so spend-ing the holiday season in Florida wasn't a sacrifice, and the extended family loved the warmer climate.

Opening the Brentwood's file before she exited her car, Charlotte double-checked her notes. Charles had retired from his engineering position and Barbara was a retired teacher. They had worked hard for everything they had, and Charlotte thoroughly enjoyed helping them on every project Barbara came up with. Charlotte was reminded of Aunt Bea from *The Andy Griffith Show* when she thought of Barbara Brentwood, and her warm and welcoming personality.

Today was an initial meeting to take measurements and talk over general ideas on the family room renovation. As she approached the Cape-style house, she recalled the previous work she had done there: traditional, with clean lines, no fuss.

An hour and a half later, Charlotte walked out of the family room with a game plan for the Brentwood project. "I love working with you on this house. This is the style I personally gravitate toward. Barbara, I'd like to set up a meeting next week. I should have some fabric swatches and furniture styles for you to look over." Vibration from her pocket alerted Charlotte to an incoming phone call. "Excuse me." She looked at who was calling. "I'm sorry. Please excuse me. I need to take this call."

"Hi Carolyn, do you have anything for me?" Charlotte listened as she walked to the foyer. "Ok, keep looking and let me know what you come up with."

Charles walked down the hallway with a tray of teacups and a plate of cookies when Charlotte turned off her cellphone. "Is everything all right?"

"I apologize for the interruption. I usually turn off my phone when I meet with clients, but I've been waiting to hear back from my realtor. This morning I modified my search parameters, and I wanted to make sure she understood the type of home I would be interested in purchasing."

"Go ahead." Charles nodded and Charlotte walked back into the room as he followed. Barbara and Charlotte took seats in front of the picture window. He poured three cups of tea. "For you Barb. Charlotte, milk? Sugar?" He passed the cups and went back to his spot by the door to stay out of the way.

Barbara looked at her husband, then back at Charlotte. "Oh, I'm sorry. I overheard you. I guess we didn't know you were moving. With small-town chit chat, we usually hear stuff."

"Long story short, Grant and I came to an understanding, and now I need to find a place to live. I'd love something to fix up and improve upon, but keep its character. This part of the county would be ideal, but I think everything is already owned or developed."

Charles pushed his weight off the doorframe and stood straight. "If you have a few minutes, I can show you a home that might have been forgotten by its owners. I take the dog for a walk in the woods near it a few times a week. It isn't rundown, so someone has been looking after it, but there's no way anyone lives in it. I confess. I've looked in the windows."

"Seriously? If you don't mind, I'd love to see it."

Charles put his German shepherd on a leash while Charlotte went to her car to unload her things and put on more sensible shoes for walking. Barbara declined the walk, but wished them luck.

Charlotte, Charles and Cooper, the dog, walked down the lane and crossed Pinewood Road. Almost immediately, Charlotte spotted the path Charles said he walked. She could tell that once upon a time, it would have been an access road or driveway, but neglect had let the brush grow over most of it.

"I can smell the leaves."

"Like I said, I think I'm up here more than the person who owns the place. I see tire tracks, but I never see anyone. It's a peaceful place, with birds chirping and squirrels and chipmunks running around. I even saw a moose once. Have to say, it scared me half to death."

Charlotte was a little startled at the idea of a moose wandering around.

They walked on for a few minutes.

"I think that at one time, this property was part of a larger farm down the hill. As you'll see, the house is on top of the hill, and from there you can easily view the land below."

The path opened. Sunlight came through the canopy above, as if shining a spotlight on the magical house in the woods. It was built in traditional saltbox colonial style, with the addition of a small roof over the front door. It appeared to have original cedar shakes and possibly original windows. Charlotte could see several fireplace chimneys, and she wondered if the house even had running water or electricity.

"I can see why you would come for walks up here. My dog would be in heaven. That is amazing." Charlotte suddenly stilled as she gazed at what appeared to be a forgotten historic landmark.

"Isn't it, though? I'd love to see you get your hands on it and make something of this old place. In the last few years, someone has been coming up here to check on things, but I've never run into him or her. I think retirement is making me nosier. Anyhow, if it's a style you like, maybe it wouldn't hurt to see if it's on the market."

They walked with Cooper around the outside of the house. At the back, Charlotte could see how the property sloped down to the farm below, but still kept a generous yard for a garden and even a patio for entertaining. She could see these things in her mind. On the far side of the property, set back and overrun by bushes, were what looked like the remnants of a chicken coop. She thought maybe it could be turned into a shed.

On the way back toward her car, Charlotte was contemplative. Charles took the dog off the leash and Cooper ran to his yard chasing a squirrel up a tree. "Do you have any idea who owns the land?"

"As long as Barb and I have lived here, that land has been vacant. I was always too busy working to be bothered to look into who owned it."

"Hmm. It is something. Thanks for taking me to see it." Charlotte said goodbye, got into her car, and drove off. The vibrating cell phone on the seat next to her alerted Charlotte to an incoming text message. Picking it up at the next stop sign she regretted the decision immediately. Looking at the text from Grant started a tension headache she wasn't sure was going to go away anytime soon.

"I'd like to take you out to dinner. We can discuss those projects."

Not on your life. "I'm sorry. I have other plans. I'm meeting ..." The idea of telling Grant she was meeting with another man eased some of that tension he had caused, even if it was a fictitious date. "Luke Anderson." *No reply. Maybe he got the hint to leave things along.*

Tossing and turning in the dark hotel room later that evening wasn't helping to bring on sleep. Opening her eyes, Charlotte counted ceiling tiles willing her restless spirit to relax. It didn't work. Thoughts of the house in the woods kept her awake. Thoughts of running her fingers along the scruffy jaw of a sexy carpenter that was helping her fix things in a house flashed to mind. Reaching to the night stand, Charlotte found her laptop and sent an e-mail to her realtor. "Can you get information on the wooded property located on Pinewood Road?"

Chapter Five

THE PARKS IS a picturesque thousand-lot subdivided development ranging from attached condominiums to two-acre parcels. It is on one of the two-acre lots that Luke found himself listening to Joe, his second in command, rant about how the general contractor was making demands on the spot for changes, without change forms, to major finish work on the kitchen space.

Waving his hands in the air. Joe threw a shop rag onto a saw horse. "So the GC says the homeowner now wants the crown to have a hand carved leaf and dentil, not just a dentil detail. I told him we would do it, but it'll cost someone, and it won't be us, since we've already installed the crown with the dentil molding."

Walking around the room and looking up, Luke inspected the work already completed. Stopping quickly, he placed his hands on his hips. "Okay, got it. Don't touch it yet, though. I don't want to hear that the homeowner had a change of heart and doesn't want the upcharge once they see the price for the teardown and reinstall."

Luke watched as Joe's eyes glanced past his shoulder, then back to him. "Fine, let me know what the next step is when you find out."

"Will do." The vibrating buzz of Luke's cellphone had him look at the incoming number. Not recognizing it, Luke sent the call to voice mail. Turning, he was surprised to see Charlotte Cavanaugh standing inside the front door.

"Well, look at you standing there, not afraid to get dusty," he said.

"Nice to see you as well. I got the impression from Aimee Martin that you worked on bigger projects, so thank you again. I guess I should be honored you've taken on this humble abode." She walked further into the house, closer to him.

Joe walked past Luke and Charlotte to head to another room. He looked Charlotte up and down from behind and smiled as he caught Luke's eye. "Morning Miss. I think I'll just go over there." He pointed with his thumb over his shoulder.

"You do that, Joe." Luke tilted his head toward the doorway for Joe to leave. "Where were we … humble abode. I like to think so, as well, even though it's not so humble. There was a lull in my own work load, so I agreed to help the guy who was scheduled to do this job. Something about his wife having a baby. Lame excuse, right?"

Luke smiled a cheesy grin that made his eyes squint and Charlotte smiled back. "Right. He should have told his wife to suck it up." They both laughed. "I didn't mean to overhear, but did your guy say that the crown in the kitchen has to be changed?"

"Something like that. I think you walked in after all the ranting and arm waving and pacing around the room. Anyhow, it's not a big deal. I'll talk with the GC and see what the story is. What are you up to here?"

"I'm here to check on progress. I'm working for the Sullivan's, the homeowners, on all the interiors of the house. Can I look at which crown is up?"

"Sure, knock yourself out."

Charlotte ran her hand along the chair rail in the hallway as they walked toward the back of the house. She frowned when she saw the crown molding that was already up around the ceiling. "I'm confused, because this is the crown that's supposed to be up there. Who said it needed to be changed? Never mind. I'll sort this out. Unless you see a change form, don't touch that crown."

"Yes, ma'am. I like a woman in charge, making decisions." Luke leaned in behind Charlotte, enjoying her choice of perfume.

She turned to face him, and he stepped back quickly. "Do you have time to show me around the rest of the house? I don't want to get in your way if it's too much trouble."

"No trouble at all." Luke waved his hand like a gameshow host. The pair walked from room to room, looking at all the detailed finish work his small crew had been carefully putting in place. The library space was where Luke had planned to spend most of his day, installing custom floor-to-ceiling shelves. His compound miter box was set up in the middle of the room. "The brass bar for the ladder to hang from already arrived. That'll add a nice touch to this room. Old world library feel."

"Mr. Anderson, you're very perceptive. That's exactly the look the homeowners want for this room. My estimation is that every one of these shelves will be filled. He has first editions of classics. Which would make some public libraries weep. Has the ladder arrived, as well?"

"Not that I'm aware of." They walked further into the house and looked in the two full and one half bathrooms. The master suite was the last room they entered. "I couldn't believe the size of this space when I walked in here." His eyes scanned the walls from floor to ceiling looking for anything that might be out of place.

She walked around the room, looking down at the installation of the wood floor. She pointed to the molding on the walls just above the floor. "That looks good. How about the cabinets in there?"

Charlotte walked past Luke and stepped into the spa-like bathroom retreat. Sunlight came through the block glass windows above the corner Jacuzzi tub, creating a halo around her. The effect highlighted her features. When she turned back to Luke, he saw the glow of her skin and the shine of her hair. The light reflected off the diamond pendant around her neck.

"… what do you think of them?" she asked, snapping him out of his reverie.

"I'm sorry. I was thinking about another project we have going. What did you say?"

"Sorry, I'm keeping you. I only said I thought the cabinets looked good and asked what you thought. I should get out of your way."

Luke leaned into the room and looked around. "I'd say my crew can check this off the list for now. The cabinets came out of a box, so it didn't take long to set them in place. The granite guys and plumber have their work, so we can't finish any minor clean up till they're done." When he stepped back Charlotte turned, and they ended up nose to nose. "Sorry. I'll just ..." he pointed to the side.

Luke stepped left. Charlotte moved to her right. "Sorry, I'll just ..." she said. Charlotte moved to her left and Luke tried to get out of her way by moving to his right. Again, they were nose to nose. To stop the dance, Luke put his hands on her shoulders.

"Miss Charlotte, I'm going to step backward now so I can get out of your way." Luke felt her body heat beneath his hands. The thought of feeling the heat from other parts of her body held him in place a fraction of a second longer.

"You were saying?" she asked.

"Yes, I'm moving now. We have a little more of the house to check out." He quickly stepped back and led the way to the parts of the house they hadn't yet visited. They walked through together, silently taking notes. On the balcony overlooking the front door, Luke watched the general contractor, Grant Becker, walk in.

He looked over at Charlotte and saw the scowl on her face. "That's the general contractor. But you probably know that. Are you not a fan of his?"

"Let's just say I've dealt with him in the past. Thank you for showing me the progress. If you'll excuse me, I'll see about that change order your guys were told was on the way."

Charlotte descended the stairs. Halfway down, she looked up and saw he still watched her. Then Luke saw that Grant had witnessed the exchange, and Luke decided he didn't want to talk with him at that moment. He stepped back from the railing so he couldn't be seen. He had a feeling this exchange would be interesting to witness. This little lady seemed like she could bust some balls. When he heard her tone change from friendly banter to commanding, Luke decided he didn't want to witness this guy's undoing. He made his way to the library to continue his work on the shelves.

***

Charlotte had noticed Grant's facial expression change when she reached the last step. She recognized the look as his salesman face. He was going to try and sweet talk her, and she was prepared. "Grant, the house is coming along nicely. I think we need to have a discussion about the crown molding in the kitchen, though." He stepped forward to give her a kiss, but she turned her face just in time.

"It's nice to see you here," he said. "A surprise, for sure. I think the crew is doing a fantastic job. Well, except for some of the finish work. I've been checking on their progress every day. I usually don't use them, but I guess there was an emergency or something with the sub we had contracted with, so he brought in these guys."

He rolled his eyes. Charlotte thought how funny it was that she'd never noticed his annoying facial expressions.

"I know the lead of that crew," she said. "Luke Anderson is a skilled carpenter. He just showed me the progress. I have to say, I don't think anything is out of order."

Straightening his back, Grant lifted his chin the slightest bit as he started to pace. "That's because they know I'm here *ALL* the time, checking up on them."

He waved his arms as he spoke, as if trying to emphasize his point. Had he always been this exasperating? Charlotte wondered how she hadn't ever noticed before today.

"I see," she said. "Well, there was a question about the molding ..."

"Can you believe they installed that crap in there? I told them they had to take it down and install the correct molding, and they were eating the cost."

Charlotte put her hands on her hips, adjusted her stance. This was her power posture, and she knew it intimidated Grant. He had even said so in the past. "Grant, what are you doing? You know as well as I do that the molding installed is the correct stuff. Hell, even Luke knows. Stop trying to find an excuse to prolong this project."

"It's not right." He pouted.

She almost laughed at him, but she wanted to wrap up this conversation and make sure he knew she was not going to go along with his games. "It is the right stuff. There's no way you're going to hand me a change order form to sign off on. I've already told Luke that unless I make the change, his guys are not to do any additional work on the molding in the kitchen. This is the end of the discussion."

"Fine, I won't make them change it. Charlotte, it's just … it's just … I want you back. I want to take you out to dinner. Say you'll go with me?"

"Not on your life, Grant." She walked out the door, around the exterior of the house, and headed to her car. When she got in behind the wheel, she could see Luke Anderson through the library window. He held his phone to his ear. His eyes squinted, causing his eyebrows to furrow. Charlotte wanted to take her pointer finger and smooth the crease out. Soothe whatever it was that gave him that concerned look. A warm and tingly sensation started to works its way up her body. She thought maybe she would drive with the windows down to clear her head and remember her new motto of "*No dating.*"

Chapter Six

WESTHAMPTON WAS AN old town with boundary
lines that went well out to the county limits. Developers
clamored to buy up as much of the old farming land as possible. It seemed that everyone wanted to move out to the sub-
urbs and was willing to pay a high price to do so. Some mid-
range developments were going up, but for the most part the
new homes were complete custom projects.

The Camden family was doing well financially, and
wanted to invest in just such a home. A few months back
they had contacted Charlotte. They had learned about her
interior work from a former client who had been extremely
pleased with the outcome of their project. Back then she was
still tightly involved with Grant, so she hadn't hesitated to
refer him to the Camden's as a general contractor.

As she sat in the meeting that morning with all the involved parties, she began second-guessing her decision.

"The plans are coming along quite well. I expect to move
quickly now that the house is dried in—that means the roof is

on. There won't be a swimming pool where the basement is."
Grant was his calm, cool self. He was showing the Camdens
that in-control guy who, just a few weeks ago, she'd thought
was amazing. Now, though, she saw the salesman and she
wanted to cringe.

Mr. Camden was an advertising executive and hadn't
been involved in a construction project before. He was right-
fully curious about the whole process. His questions were
thought-out and to the point. "What kind of contingencies
are worked in for weather delays? Does a delay like this affect
our budget? Our budget is set so nothing can change that,
right?"

"Weather delays are worked in when planning a project.
For a house of this size, I've allowed for seven days of delay
for this time of year. I've overestimated that." Grant winked
at Mrs. Camden. "The basement is dug, framing is done, and
the roof is on. That's all the big stuff. The plumbers, electri-
cians, heating and air conditioning guys will do their part.
Then the dry wall guys will cover it all to make the rooms.
That's when it'll start to feel like a house, when you can really
see the room sizes. At this point, the nitty-gritty of the project
gets underway, and Ms. Cavanaugh starts to work her magic."

Charlotte spoke up. This wasn't her part to talk, but she
wanted to make sure the Camdens were reassured. "Unless
you make a major change to the overall plans, your budget is
set. Now, when we get to the interior design side, we'll have
to work out a new budget and stay within that. I know you
have three kids, so we'll try not to break into their college
funds." Everyone laughed.

"But you'll stick to the budget, right?"

"Of course, Mr. Camden. Once you and your wife settle on the interior budget, I'll work within that. Unless, of course, you decide you can live without a home theater. That will free up a lot of the budget for your wife."

Mr. Camden looked around the room. "Yes, the theater should go. We can use that space for storage."

"He's a practical man." The sound of Grant laughing louder than everyone else grated on Charlotte's nerves. Her head throbbed and she rubbed her temple to ease the ache.

The rest of the meeting went just like all other construction meetings Charlotte had with Grant and clients. Grant presented the Camdens with the final plans of their dream home and talked them through the process. A lengthy discussion started when Mr. Camden questioned the need for two separate heating and air conditioning systems. To his credit, Grant was knowledgeable about the necessity of the dual systems. "With a house this size, it ends up being more efficient to have two zones with separate systems. Your main living space doesn't need to be heated during the day, because the family is at school or working. Your home office is in another zone, which you would want heated since you'll be using that space. Why have heat where you won't be using it? Does that make sense?"

"But that will cost more, right?"

Grant was thoughtful in clarifying things for Mr. Camden. "Sure, the system and the installation cost will be more. In the long run it will save you money not heating or cooling areas of the home you won't be in at certain times."

Mrs. Camden put her hand on her husband's arm. "I think that makes sense." He nodded and she continued. "I guess we'll leave that for the professionals." She looked around the room. "He's under a lot of stress at work." Mrs. Camden held her husband's hand. "So, all of the decisions have been made until everything is dried in? That's the correct term, right?

Grant looked pleased with himself, and Charlotte couldn't help but feel pleased as well. The Camden family was very nice, and to help them bring their dream home to life was personally satisfying. She gathered her papers on the desk to get ready to leave for her next meeting.

"Ms. Cavanaugh, I have a few questions about another project. Can you stick around a minute?"

"Sure thing, Mr. Becker. Mr. and Mrs. Camden, I'll be in touch soon with some fabric samples for the living room." Grant walked the couple to the conference room door, and she waved to them as they left the room.

"Charlotte, do you have time to meet for lunch today?"

"I have a meeting I'm heading to right now, and I'm not sure how long that will last. Is there something I can help you with quick, or do we need to set up a time?"

He reached out and held her hand. "I want us to have lunch. Like we always do. Is that so hard?"

Charlotte pulled her hand back and wrinkled her brow. "Um, Grant, I think I need some clarification. Did you just ask me out to lunch, like a date?"

"I need to see you, be with you, Charlotte. I made a mistake, and I hate the thought of you going home to an empty house."

Charlotte put the last of her things in her bag. She grabbed her jacket off the back of her chair and put it on.

With her things in hand, she looked directly at Grant. "The funny thing is I'm not the least bit interested in seeing you socially. You're very good at what you do professionally, and I do admire your work. But what I've come to realize is that the connection we had must not have been very real, or I would have been crushed by your betrayal. I'm not crushed. I'm over it." She walked to the door and turned to face him once more. "It was nice, Grant, don't get me wrong. I don't regret our time together. I think maybe we just went past our expiration date."

Grant stared daggers at her. This was a man who was used to getting his way. "It was *nice?* You're such a bitch. Maybe if you'd have been a better lover, I wouldn't have strayed."

Charlotte took a deep breath, then put her hand up. "I'll be in touch when I need an update." She was livid with Grant, but refused to argue back. She was moving on and letting him get under her skin wasn't going to help.

Charlotte walked out the office door, down the hall, and then practically hopped down the stairs. Being able to speak her mind to Grant had liberated her in a way she hadn't expected.

Released from a bond she didn't know held her down she felt free and light, and wanted to share the news. The pain she felt earlier in her head was gone, and Charlotte laughed at the idea of her body responding to being around Grant in a very real, pain in the head kind of way. Unfortunately, everyone she called from her car was either in a meeting or on the phone. Spur of the moment, she called her parents. She drove down Steward Street and stopped at a red light. Her mother answered at the same time Charlotte realized Aimee's brother Jim's bar was across the street.

"Hi Mom. Listen, I'll have to call you back. I have a meeting I'm walking into, but I have some news to share. No, I don't have time this second, but I'll call in a little while. Love you. Bye."

She put her blinker on to turn left and then parked in the bar's parking lot. The open sign was lit, and only one motorcycle and a big truck could be seen. "What the heck." She got out of her car and walked around to the front door. She had just been here with Aimee, but she couldn't remember being in the parking lot. The building and lot were well maintained. In the windows, neon signs advertised beer. The exterior paint wasn't chipping, and nothing screamed "biker bar" at her. The other night when she read the menu it stated lunch was served daily, so she went in.

It took a few seconds for her eyes to adjust to the darkened interior, but when she did she noticed Jim behind the bar, talking to a guy who had his back to her. Jim looked up. "Well, look what the cat dragged in. Nice to see you again so soon." That was when the guy on the barstool turned.

***

Luke had just finished typing a text to his realtor inquiring about the status of his grandmother's house, which was for sale, when he saw Charlotte standing near the bar entrance. He wanted to lean over and kiss Jim on the lips for owning the place. He had been thinking about the raven-haired beauty since their tour of the Sullivan house. "Well, Jim, someone has to make this place look better."

She walked like a runway model. This was the third time he'd been near her, and the third time he was getting to see another pair of sky-high heels that supported legs with calf muscles that begged for him to touch. Luke started to wonder if it had been too long since he'd been with someone because he was thinking even her toes were sexy, peeping out of the front of those shoes. Well, he thought, the whole picture in front of him was sexy as hell.

"I think the cat dragged you in here first, Luke." Charlotte placed her hand on his shoulder, leaned in and kissed Jim on the cheek. It was a familiar, confident move. Luke thought it must be the way she greeted friends.

"Take a load off there, Charlotte. What can I get you?" Jim stood with his hands on the bar top, taking in the beauty before him. Luke wanted to push him away and tell him to back off. He knew he had no reason to feel this way, other than the fact Charlotte made him feel things he hadn't felt in a very long time.

She pointed to Luke's cola. "One of those."

Luke was surprised at her choice of drink. He had her pegged as a diet girl. "Not that either of us is objecting, but this isn't your regular hangout spot. What's up?" He gestured to the coke Jim put in front of Charlotte. "That's on me, Jim."

Charlotte lifted the drink and tilted it toward Luke. "Thanks." She took a long pull on it and, in a very unladylike fashion, wiped her top lip with the back of her hand. "To answer your question, I had a great meeting with a crappy ending. It's lunchtime. I happened to be driving by, and saw the open sign. I was just looking for a familiar face."

"And here you found two." Jim indicated Luke and himself.

The phone rang on the other end of the bar. "I'll be right back," Jim turned and walked past the rows of bottles showcased in front of a mirror. He stopped just under a spotlight that cast a soft glow, just enough light for him to find the phone.

Luke watched Charlotte take another drink. "So, what are you doing going into a bar in the middle of the day?"

"I just left a meeting and felt down and out. I was about to confess to my mother that I'm homeless when I think I had an epiphany, or I saw the bar and decided to stop. One of the two happened."

"Do you want to talk about it?"

"No … yes. He's such a dickhead. He, my ex, cheated on me and now he's pissy because I don't want to be with him. Now he's like, you'll regret not being with me. He's acting worse than a teenage girl with PMS and no prom date."

Luke was surprised by her fiery words. "I guess taking a load off and venting will help you focus for that next appointment?"

She blushed and looked down at her glass. "Sorry. I usually do handle my emotions better. Grant got the better of me today."

"Whoa, Grant Becker is your ex? That explains a few things."

Sitting straighter, she pulled her shoulders back. Milliseconds passed and a mask appeared over her features;

she pursed her lips before speaking. "What does that mean exactly?" she asked.

"I think I might've just stepped in it. What I should have said was that when we were at the end of our tour of the Sullivan house, and Becker walked in and saw me talking to you, he shot daggers at me. I thought it was just because he's the boss and I'm just a laborer and should have been working. Now I think he might have been jealous you were talking to another man. I apologize if my comment offended you."

"Apology accepted." Charlotte flashed him a dazzling smile. "If me being with you on that job site got him upset, then I like it."

Her cellphone chirped and she laughed. "That's my realtor's ringtone. I should get that."

"Have at it."

Charlotte didn't step away from the bar, so Luke didn't feel like he was intruding on her call. He took a sip of his coke and listened to the one-sided conversation. The buzzing vibrating of his own cellphone on the bar top caught Luke's attention. He picked up his phone and looked at the text, deleted it and set the phone back down. He decided he didn't want to look at it, so he put his phone in his pocket. Charlotte ended her call and took another sip.

"Do you have plans tomorrow?" she asked him. "What am I thinking? Of course you have plans. You're a busy guy. What I meant to ask was whether you had time tomorrow to check out a property with me? I inquired about an older home for sale on some land outside the city limits. I'd like another opinion about its soundness."

Reaching for his phone again, Luke searched his calendar. "I can do that. Why don't we grab some food and then head out to this house? Let's say we meet at Gloria's Diner around 11:30. I have a three o'clock meeting I need to attend."

"Great. I'll let my realtor know." She sent off a quick text.

Chatting about other jobs they both had in the works created an easy flow between them that Luke enjoyed. Jim was still talking on his phone at the other end of the bar. It surprised Luke when his cellphone buzzed again. He picked it up and read the text. *Potential buyer for your family homestead.* Well, that information was interesting. Luke thought it was purely a coincidence that Charlotte was looking at a house, and he was selling one.

"I need to make a call. It was nice seeing you." He put some money on the bar and pointed to her coke. "I've got that one, remember?"

"I can buy my own drink."

He looked her right in the eye. "I said I got it."

"Ok. I'll see you tomorrow, Luke."

He raised his hand to signal to Jim he was leaving. "Tomorrow." He put on his jacket as he walked to the door. He caught Charlotte watching him. "See ya."

Chapter Seven

TWO SPOTS REMAINED in Gloria's Diner parking lot. It was packed. Luke parked his Ford in a spot and walked toward the diner. He spotted Charlotte in a booth by the window and noticed she wasn't alone. Grant Becker sat opposite her. Even from this distance, he could tell Charlotte didn't look happy. She sat straight up, arms crossed, and her lips pursed like she ate a lemon. Luke decided he was going to step in to rescue her.

He told the hostess he was meeting someone and saw Charlotte visibly relax when she noticed him approaching the table. Grant's head turned, following her gaze. He must have noticed the slight smile on those soft lips of hers and known it hadn't been for him.

Pulling out all the stops, he decided to act the part of the courting southern gentleman and laid it on thick with his accent. "Sorry I've kept you, baby girl." He leaned over and kissed her on the lips. He closed his eyes, savoring the moment.

By her initial quick breath, he wasn't sure if she'd caught on to his act, but he was the one who ended up being surprised when she reached up and put her hand behind his neck, holding him in place a few more seconds. Luke opened his eyes. He enjoyed the view of Charlotte up close and more relaxed than he'd ever seen her. Her eyes had been closed as well, but then her lashes fluttered and he looked into her copper eyes. He couldn't help but see the dreaminess reflected back at him.

"Hi yourself. I've been waiting. I think Grant was just about to leave."

Luke sat down next to Charlotte, and to make the show for Grant even more over-the-top, he took a sip of Charlotte's water and held her hand.

Grant stood up and spoke in what sounded like a loud whisper. "I don't know what kind of game you're playing, Charlotte, but you're going to be sorry. Your client list is going to dry up. They only used you because I referred them." He left the diner in a huff, pushing the door with both hands.

"Wow, he seems to have some pent-up aggression. I wonder if things aren't working out with him and his secretary." Her toothy smile reached her eyes and she laughed. It was a great full laugh.

Luke couldn't help it. He laughed out loud. A few of the other diners looked over. He gave them a small wave and then turned back to Charlotte, blocking out the rest of the room. "You're something. What do you say we order lunch and then go take a look at the house?" He got out of the booth and slid in the seat across from her. His truck keys landed on the table with a thud from the load of keys on the ring; he placed his cell phone next to them.

The waitress flipped her order pad to an empty page. "What can I get for you kids?" They kept it simple and she left.

Luke ordered a sweet tea to drink, and Charlotte decided she would try it. "I've found since moving north, a lot of places don't have sweet tea so I get it when I can."

"So Luke, what brought you to New England from down south? Georgia?"

"This is where my momma's from. Over the years I came to visit a few times, and it held a magical quality for me. You know what I mean?" He wasn't sure he could explain any better than that. "Anyhow, my family's been in the construction industry for a very long time. They started building barns for farmers when my great grandfather was bored with his farm. He decided he didn't want the farm any longer and only wanted to build things. The problem with his decision was that the farm was in my grandmother's family. They made a deal that she would run the farm and he would run the construction business. If either one couldn't keep their end going, it would be sold off."

Their food arrived and they began to eat. Luke's phone vibrated on the table.

Charlotte pointed to the phone as she took a sip of tea. "You going to answer that?"

"Nope. I think someone has the wrong number, and they keep calling to harass me. Maybe if I ignore it they'll go away."

"I hope so for your sake. So back to your move here. Your story still doesn't explain the connection to here," Charlotte said as she ate.

"That story is kind of lengthy. How about we finish up here and as we look around the house, I'll share it."

"Deal."

The waitress brought the check. Luke grabbed it and stood to go to the cash register. Charlotte stood as well, slipping on a jacket. Luke noticed she was dressed in jeans and hiking boots. *Looks like she wants to get to know the property*, he thought.

It had to be a coincidence that he was selling a house and she was buying. He brushed the absurd idea aside and tuned in his favorite country station on the satellite radio. Charlotte turned right, he followed. Another song started and her car turned right again. He followed again. The roads were all too familiar. Charlotte's car slowed to a stop as she turned onto a tree-lined drive. He knew it wasn't just a coincidence.

Luke thought about how to explain to Charlotte that he is the true owner of the house. He wasn't quite sure how he was going to tell her. When his mother was in the hospital, before she passed away, she'd made him promise that if he had to sell the property for any reason, it had to be to the right person. In the back of his mind, he knew Charlotte was the right person, but he was waiting for her to prove it. Luke wanted to hear about the plans she would have for renovating the old place. Maybe then he would tell her about owning it? He would when the time was right.

***

Charlotte turned her Mercedes off the main road and drove up the long, winding drive first. Luke followed in his truck. The tall pines and maples made a canopy, shading the way up toward the home. She rolled down the window so she could listen to the enchanting sounds of the woods around her. To her surprise, she crossed a small bridge over a babbling brook before starting up a slight incline. She could hear the crunch of dried leaves beneath the tires of her car. The top of the road leveled out, and around a bend she saw an opening in the trees. Sitting there, in the middle of a flat piece of land, was the house she hoped to call her home.

She stopped in the circular drive right at the front door, but didn't immediately get out of the car. She sat studying the façade. It was truly amazing for the house to be in such magnificent shape after all these years of not having a resident. She caught a glimpse of Luke getting out of his truck in her rearview mirror. He turned to pull some gloves from the truck storage and tuck them into the back pocket of his jeans. That tingly feeling was back. She had the perfect view of his formfitting jeans, which made her want to slide her own hand into that pocket. *Back to the house, Charlotte.*

She stepped out of the car, enjoying the peaceful surroundings. The house sat in the middle of a field of tall grasses surrounded by white birch, pine and maple trees. The landscaping had been neglected, but the potential for an abundant perennial garden was there. Charlotte turned in a full circle taking in her surroundings. Chirping birds, rustling leaves and a squirrel dashing out from the underbrush reminded her of a fairy tale. The small animal spotted her, stood tall holding onto the acorn it had found, sniffed the air and then ran back the way it had come.

Luke met Charlotte at the bottom steps, which led to the red front door. "Do you have the code for the lockbox?"

"I do. I was surprised when the realtor said I could just walk around the house by myself." She shrugged. "I guess they'll just change the code on the box after we leave." Charlotte pulled out the slip of paper on which she had written the combination for the lockbox and spun the dial to the correct places. She pulled out the key, unlocked the front door and went inside.

"Oh my goodness." She took a few seconds to absorb what she was seeing. The space opened to a large foyer. To the right were French doors with blown-glass panels. To the left was a large, leaded glass window overlooking the yard at the side of the house. Straight in front of them was a wonderfully grand staircase with a maple handrail, which ran down to the bottom step and ended in a simply stated swirling end post. Each spindle was made of maple, as well as the treads on each step leading to the second floor. The wide-plank, hardwood flooring was aged, but not particularly worn. In awe of the craftsmanship, Charlotte whispered, "Houses aren't built with so much detail anymore."

"No, they aren't. Let's take a look around. I want to hear what kind of plans you can see yourself making."

"The floors. I can't get over the floors."

Charlotte felt Luke watching her. She turned at the sound of his voice.

"You're walking on a combination of maple and walnut," he said. "I always find it fascinating to see how carpenters back then crafted a building."

"It's beautiful." She ran her hand along the glass doorknob. It was like a hand sized piece of a crystal chandelier, cool to the touch and surprisingly smooth. "Let's go see what else we can find."

The two walked from room to room. Luke pointed out the antique light bulbs mounted into the wood beam ceiling of the sitting room. Charlotte discovered a surprise room off the far side of the house. It was a porch enclosed with windows. "This would have a lovely view of those flowerbeds in the spring." She pointed toward the far side of the yard. She surprised him with her vision for the large area, which was currently full of weeds.

The kitchen was large and considerably outdated. "This would need some updating. Do you think the wiring in the house is within code?"

"I'm not an electrician, but if you do any major renovations you might have to change the entire service to carry the load. It might not be a bad idea to do a service change anyhow. The house wasn't built with WiFi in mind." Charlotte noticed Luke make a note in a pad he pulled out of his pocket. She thought it was kind of him to be taking notes for her.

She followed him past an archway and realized it must be the pantry. He stepped to the side to let Charlotte pass. Being that close to Luke in the confined space was making her internal temperature rise. "I think I need to keep moving. Claustrophobia." She lied.

Luke stepped out of the small space and Charlotte followed. She was watching his butt as he walked to the next room. He stopped and turned, and Charlotte knew she had been caught ogling him. He just smiled. "This is the private space for the domestic of the house." He must have noticed the puzzled look on her face. "Probably the room for either the maid or the cook, or maybe the person who did both jobs. You know, like Alice from *The Brady Bunch*."

They both laughed. Charlotte felt the awkward tension break, and they continued the tour of the interior of the house. They walked up the back staircase to the second floor. More detail work on that level to enjoy, as well.

Inside the walk-in closet of the smallest bedroom was another door, which led to the attic room. Charlotte quickly walked up the finished stairs and noted the large space, with a solid floor and proper lighting, as well as windows in the dormers. On the way down, she commented to Luke, "This attic could easily be turned into an additional room, like a studio or craft space."

"Are you one of those crafty ladies?"

"Um, no, but I could be."

They both smiled. Charlotte wasn't crafty because she didn't have the time. It was one of those things she would like to do, but didn't make a priority.

"I should probably see the cellar. I just hope there aren't any mice. I can deal with a lot of icky things, but mice freak me out."

"Charlotte, I hate to say it, but there're going to be a lot more menacing things to deal with out here than field mice."

Raising her shoulders and shaking her head, Charlotte mocked a shiver. "Eek. Do you do house calls to exterminate?"

"I can if you're nice to me." He raised his eyebrows up and down. "Come on, chicken."

They proceeded down the creaky stairs. Luke turned and held out his hand. The last four steps were steep, and she didn't want to lose her balance. Still holding her hand, he pulled the chain that turned on the exposed light bulbs hanging from the floor joists.

"It's a dirt cellar," he explained. "I believe it was standard for the time this house was built. Winter vegetables would do well here. You know, turnip, squash that kind of stuff."

"I'll take your word for that," Charlotte said. "My green thumb stops at daffodils and geraniums. I guess I should learn some of this stuff if I'm going to live on my own outside the town limits. Okay, let's get out of here and check out the yard." Luke let go of her hand. The loss of the comfort he had given her in the damp cellar surprised her. Charlotte gladly went up the stairs ahead of him though, away from any potential creepy crawlies.

With the second floor interior and the cellar fully appreciated, Charlotte led the way to the back of the house. They went out the door off the kitchen and began to walk around the property.

"Are you sure you wouldn't feel too isolated living this far out?"

Charlotte turned in a circle and took in her surroundings: the beautifully kept historic home, the mature trees, the chicken coop, the overgrown landscaping. "This is exactly what I want. At work, my office is my space to escape to when I need to think about the next step in a project or prepare for the next client meeting. I want—no, strike that—I need this. It's completely removed from that hustle-and-bustle world where everything is rushed and has time constraints. This is a home. When I want to be secluded, I can be. When I want to host a party, well, it's big enough to do that, as well. I want to be able to spend my time in each room to bring it back to its full potential." She slid her hand into her jeans pocket and pulled out her cellphone. "As a matter of fact, I think I need to talk to my realtor to put in an offer." She found the number and hit dial.

"I need to mention something …"

She held up a finger for Luke to wait a second. "Hi, I'm at the house and love it. I know it's quick, but I want to put in an offer." Charlotte moved away from Luke to pace across the backyard. When she turned, she noticed his pinched eyebrows and the way he was running his hand through his hair. Her realtor caught her attention again and they discussed the offer.

Luke approached her when she disconnected the call. "Well, that was quick."

"I told her to write up the offer and I'd be over to sign it. No need to wait on things. Living in that hotel is getting old, and I love this place. There's a history here, and I would love to be the one to uncover it." Her phone rang. "Sorry, I turned the ringer back on. It's the office, I should take it."

"I think …"

Charlotte held up a finger. "Let me take this. I'll call you later."

Luke reached for Charlotte's hand before she stepped too far away. "How about we go have a drink? I think I need to talk with you about something."

"That would be wonderful. We can celebrate when they accept my offer." She opened her car door and Luke held it while she got in.

"Sure, give me a call." Luke closed the door for her.

***

This is just great, he thought to himself. He mentally kicked himself for not telling her about the house's history. Luke found his realtor's phone number on his cell phone and connected the call. "Hi, it's Luke Anderson. When the offer comes in to buy the house go ahead and accept the offer. This is who I want to sell it to."

Chapter Eight

BECAUSE YOU JUST never know how a blind date will go, Charlotte drove herself to the restaurant. She waited in the bar and sent a text to Jessica. *Your cousin Kent better not be a complete dweeb.*

Jessica wrote back. *Would I ever set you up with a dweeb? Seriously? I know you would fire me in a heartbeat.*

I would not, so stop being so dramatic. I needed to eat anyway, so this works out fine. Who knows, right? He's here. Ttyl.

Kent Simon was a wonderful surprise. He escorted Charlotte to their reserved table and pulled out the chair for her. "Would you like wine with dinner?" Picking up the wine menu, Kent began scanning the list. She realized she had lumped Kent into the dweeb category simply by assuming that, since he was an accountant, it would make him a boring person. Their conversation flowed nicely, without any of the typical first-date awkward silences.

The waiter brought out the soup course and Charlotte noticed Kent looking around the room.

"Are you looking for someone?" she asked him.

He cleared his throat. "No, no. I, um, was just looking to see who was here."

"Oh, I thought Jessica said you were just in town on business. I didn't realize you knew anyone else in the area."

"Well, you see ..."

Movement in her peripheral vision alerted Charlotte to a commotion of a woman rushing toward their table with a very angry expression.

She stopped and glared down at Kent with a passing scowl at Charlotte. In a loud stage whisper, she said, "Kent Simon, I am so disappointed in you. I cannot believe you would stoop so low as to spy on me. I'm so thankful my business meeting ended before you caused a bigger scene." She looked at Charlotte again. "Come on, we're leaving." She pulled on Kent's arm with a death grip to his bicep, and he stood.

"Well, Charlotte, it was very nice to meet you." He went to pull out his wallet.

Charlotte waved at him to put it away. "That won't be necessary. I think you'll have an interesting enough end to your evening." She watched as Kent was led away by the demanding woman.

Her cellphone dinged a text message. *What happened to getting drinks?* Luke. Charlotte's instincts told her he would never have allowed her to be set up. A twinge of guilt fluttered to life. Having drinks with him sounded much more fun than sitting alone in a restaurant having dinner.

She texted him back: *Funny thing. I got set up on a blind date, and his significant other just showed up. Go figure.*

Sounds like a winner.

"You have no idea," she said out loud. *It wasn't going to go anywhere anyhow. Sorry about bailing on our drink. Another time?*

How about right now? Look over at the bar.

Luke stood at the entrance to the bar with his cellphone held up high. She laughed and waved him over. When he smiled and started to approach her table she felt a warm tug at the thought of spending more time with him.

Holding his hands up in surrender, he radiated confidence. "I promise I wasn't following you. I happened to be waiting for my friend and his wife when I spotted you. They just got here." He sat down in the now vacant seat.

"I need to apologize to you." Suddenly the room grew warm and she didn't need to see herself to know she was blushing, badly. "This dinner," she waved her hand, "I was doing a favor for a friend I work with."

"You don't owe me an apology. Nothing was set in stone. Since you seem to now be free, how about you join us? Or we could join you? What do you say? I can't guarantee it, but it might be more fun than eating alone." He flashed her a charming smile, and she could swear he was batting his ridiculously long eyelashes.

"I bet that look has gotten you into a lot of bedrooms over the years," she said. "I don't know a woman alive who would be able to turn that down."

"Is it working?" He batted his eyelashes again.

Charlotte batted at his arm for teasing her. "Why don't you have your friends come over here so you don't have to wait for a table?"

Before she knew it, Luke had picked up her hand and tenderly kissed the back of it. "I'll go tell the hostess we'll be joining you and get them from the bar. I'll be right back." He walked away.

The warm tug was ramping up, and Charlotte realized she was fanning her face. Here she was with a genuine good guy, but she had vowed to herself she was swearing off men. The aftermath of her relationship with Grant had brought about the demise of not only what she perceived as her future husband, but her future children, future life. That reality changed and this new go-with-the-flow attitude had kicked in. She hadn't expected Luke Anderson to make her question her new decisions so quickly.

Luke escorted the lovely couple back to the table and introduced them as Joe and Stella Griffin. "Joe is my second-in-command at work."

Charlotte studied Joe for a second as they all took their seats. The dress shirt and pants didn't look familiar. The salt and pepper hair and glasses hit the mark. "Did I see you at one of my houses recently?"

"I was working at the house where Luke did the walk-through with you. Thank you for letting us crash at your table. It would've been a long wait."

"My pleasure. I seem to have a lot more time on my hands now that my date's other half showed up to take him away."

Stella and Joe burst out laughing. Stella covered her mouth. "Sorry. We thought we had issues." She looked sheepish.

Joe looked at his wife. "We don't have issues. We just don't have a kitchen."

Stella rolled her eyes at her husband. "Contractors. Their own homes are always the last to get worked on."

The waiter brought over Charlotte's meal and the rest of the table insisted she start eating. She ate slowly after they'd placed their orders. While her new dinner companions talked, she noted that, for the first time in a very long time, she was able to just sit and enjoy herself in an easy, comfortable manner as the evening progressed.

"So, Charlotte, tell me about your design business. What's it like to work with these knuckleheads?" Stella had a twinkle in her eye that clearly showed her affection for not only her husband, but for Luke as well.

While they ate, Charlotte told Stella about the pros and cons of working in the design industry and being a bossy female on a jobsite. "Guys who don't know me make an assumption when they see a skirt and heels. You know, the 'this chick don't know crap about construction' assumption. They might even use more colorful words. I usually make it clear when they've screwed up—with a hammer in the wall they need to relocate or a visual just as dramatic. I get my point across."

Stella coughed holding in a mouthful of food. Charlotte knew the idea of a petite brunette telling a construction crew how to work was a funny idea. "I'd love to see you telling Joe to change something. I can just see him walking away, shaking his head and grumbling."

"Actually," Charlotte said, looking at the two gentlemen who were now her dinner companions, "these two and their

co-workers saved my timeline on that house. More im-
portantly, they saved money by double-checking on changes
they were told to make. Proper change orders hadn't been
done. That kind of diligence I appreciate and remember when
other projects come along."

Charlotte looked over at Luke and realized he'd been
watching her. He nodded. "Thank you, Charlotte. Joe and I
have a great crew."

"You're welcome, but I'm just stating the facts. Enough
shoptalk. Stella, did you see the new shops they're putting in
on Main Street?"

Luke ate as Charlotte and Stella chatted. The two women
who had just met kept a conversation going about anything
that came to mind.

Joe nudged Luke's arm. "Can you believe these two?" He
waved his hand in his wife's direction. "They just met like an
hour ago, and they're acting like long-lost friends."

"It must be a female thing."

"Must be. I was thinkin' ... have you heard anything
about the sale of your grandmother's place?"

Luke glanced across the table. Charlotte and Stella were
still consumed by their conversation about a new spa that had
just opened.

"I do have news about that. I'll tell you later." Luke tilted
his head to indicate the ladies at the table.

"Oooh, suspicious. I guess I'll just have to wait."

Stella looked over. "Wait for what?"

"I've got a hot date I need to get ready for," Joe said.
"You done talking nail polish or gossiping?"

Stella laughed at her husband. "Let's get the check so you can prepare for your hot date with the remote and the Sox."

"All taken care of. My treat," Luke said.

A round of thanks came from the table as Joe and Stella stood. Luke stood as well, accepting a hug from Stella and a handshake from Joe. "See you in the morning."

Charlotte stood, too, placing the napkin from her lap on the table. "It was very nice meeting both of you. Thank you for joining me."

Stella turned to Charlotte. "It was our pleasure. I'll give you a call to go over what we talked about."

Joe put his arm around his wife's shoulders. "Oh boy, I better get her out of here before she starts redesigning my entire house! Nice to officially meet you." He turned to Luke again. "Catch up with you tomorrow, man."

After they left, Charlotte turned to Luke. "You didn't have to buy my dinner."

"I did. Come on, I'll walk you out to your car." He waited while Charlotte picked up her handbag. Luke placed his hand on Charlotte's lower back to guide her out of the restaurant. She liked having him next to her.

Charlotte led the way to her car. "I'm parked over there."

***

Was it the lighting in the parking lot? Luke couldn't be sure. Charlotte looked up at him and he felt a jolt right down to his toes. He could tell all evening she'd been having a good time, joining in the conversation and laughing along with Joe and Stella. But this look. This was meant only for him.

"Lead the way," he said.

The lights blinked as she depressed the key fob to unlock her car. She opened the door and put her bag inside, then turned and placed her hand on the door frame. "Thank you for this evening. I did have a great time."

"That guy's poor choice in companions was my gain. I hate being Joe's third wheel, but I always enjoy their company. So thank you for saying you'd let us join you."

Before he knew what was happening, Charlotte put her hand behind his neck and pulled him down. He felt her soft, full lips on his. He watched her eyes open as she stepped back. Even in the shadowed parking lot, Luke was almost positive he saw a blush work its way up her face. She turned and got into her car before he could even move a muscle.

"Good night, Luke Anderson." Charlotte shut her car door.

The car started beside him, and Luke stepped away so she could back out of the parking space. He watched her drive off, and for a second he thought about doing a fist pump like a goofy teenager.

"Good night, Charlotte Cavanaugh."

Chapter Nine

"I SHOULD CALL her, right? It'd be the gentlemanly thing to do." Luke paced along the sidewalk. Joe sat on the back steps of the house they were working on, taking a break when Luke had walked out in his current agitated state.

"Dude, you need to chill out. Guys don't always have to do the calling nowadays." Joe took a drink from his water bottle.

"Yes, I do. My ma always told me that one of the things that women like the most is a guy with manners. You know, hold a door and let a lady walk in first. Help a lady out of a car by taking here hand. Hold an umbrella over her head so her hair doesn't get mussed up. All that kind of shit."

"This is New England man. If you start to act all gentlemanly on her, she's gonna think you're some serial killer. Girls round here don't know what a guy with manners is all about."

"Joe, you're an idiot. I have no idea what Stella sees in you."

"Man, get your panties outta your ass. If you are so
tongue tied then get a drink and just call her and get it over
with." Joe walked back into the house mumbling about his
good friend needing to get laid.

Luke walked to his truck and pulled a bottle of cold water from his cooler and sat down on the tailgate. Charlotte is
the strong, independent spirit he knew would make him
happy. He wasn't sure that he could make her happy. Luke
saw with his own two eyes how loving someone wasn't
enough to keep them in your life. Eventually, everyone either
left you alone or died. Looking up to the puffy clouds he
squinted into the sun. If Charlotte would just make the decision for him he could go with the flow. At least for a little
while. He pulled out his cellphone and stared at it willing it to
ring. It did.

"Luke Anderson" Luke listened while the supplier told
him about the delivery he had been waiting on for another
project. "That sounds great. I'll have someone over there to
accept the delivery tomorrow. I appreciate the call." He hung
up and didn't let time slip by any further. He found
Charlotte's number in his contact list and the phone started
to ring.

"Charlotte Cavanaugh Designs. This is Jessica, how may
I direct your call?"

At the sound of her voice Luke got tongue tied. "Ugh, I
was calling for Ms. Cavanaugh. This is Luke Anderson."

"Mr. Anderson, Ms. Cavanaugh is on the phone at the
moment. Would you like to leave a message in her voice
mail?"

"Ugh, no just let her know that I called."

"I will. Have a good afternoon."

"Thanks." Luke disconnected and hit his forehead with the palm of his other hand. *That was smooth*, he muttered to himself.

Frustrated that he couldn't seem to think straight when it came to thinking about one petite interior designer, Luke decided to focus his energy on his current project and headed back to his miter saw to finish cutting the corner pieces for the trim he was installing.

Installation moved along quickly and easily once he set his mind to work. The light was flashing on his cell phone to indicate a missed call or text message, so Luke stopped cleaning up his work space and checked the screen. It was a missed call from Charlotte. He wanted to kick himself for missing the call. The time stamp indicated only ten minutes after he called her, which meant he was using his saw at the time and that's why he didn't hear the phone ringing. Listening to Charlotte's relaxed, easy tone eased his tension. *Hi Luke. Sorry I missed your call. I was on a conference call with a client. I'm in the office all day with a client meeting later in the day. If you needed something just let Jessica know and she can probably take care of it. I hope to catch up with you soon. Have a great day. Oh, it's Charlotte.* The voice mail message disconnected. Finishing a few things on his punch list for the day became his priority. He decided to concentrate on that instead of the missed call.

Quiet from the other rooms signaled the rest of his crew had gone home. His watch indicated he had been alone for more than an hour. Luke pulled his earbuds, wound the cords around his iPod and moved toward his toolbox. Clattering metal surprised him, and he ran to the top of the staircase to

look for where the noise had come from. Below, he noticed a
saw on the floor and the front door wide open. "Anyone
here?" No answer. Curious he walked down and shut the
door. The dusty floor revealed several footprints. Most he
attributed to his work crew. One set stuck out, though, with
large enough print for a man's shoe that didn't make a tread.
Possibly a dress shoe. Maybe it was the homeowner checking
things out. Luke pushed the thought aside and locked the
door. Securing the worksite was the last thing he usually did
before leaving any job. Tonight he decided he would secure it
now, and again after he finished putting away his own tools.

Impulsive, knee-jerk, he wasn't sure what to call it. Luke
did it anyway. He called Charlotte knowing it was late, but he
took the chance that she would still be at her office. The
voicemail system picked up the call and indicated that the office was closed and he could press one to leave a message for
her. Luke decided that it might seem a little creepy if he left a
message after already having left a message, and he didn't
have anything to talk with her about other than he just
wanted to hear her voice, so he hung up.

He could be overthinking things, too.

Luke secured and locked the worksite later than he had
anticipated. Just up the street he saw the golden arches. He
drove through McDonald's to get something to eat and on a
whim decided to get a caramel sundae; but he ordered two.
An intersection on the way home forced him to make a decision. He could either go straight ahead or take a left to get
home. The light was red and he grabbed a few French fries
from the bag as he contemplated which direction to go. The

light turned green and he turned left, the direction that would take him right past Charlotte's hotel.

It was late when he arrived at her hotel. If she was in a house, he would have been able to see if lights were on. Instead, he reached for the cardboard cup holder that contained the two sundaes and headed inside and to the elevator.

Deciding he had gone this far, he knocked on the door. Charlotte opened the door and Luke lifted the ice cream. "I thought you might like a treat after a long day working."

"Hi ... um." She looked down at her fleece shorts and oversized sweatshirt. "Thank you. If you don't mind me looking like a bum, you are more than welcome to come in instead of standing in the hall eating your ice cream."

"I was in the drive-thru and wanted something sweet after I ate, and I was headed home and knew I would be passing. So I just thought I'd take a chance that you were here and would like a treat, too." Luke pulled his baseball cap off his head as Charlotte took the cardboard carrier from him. She waved him into the hotel room.

"Shall we sit at the table?" The bed was covered with file folders and papers and fabric swatches. "I was just getting myself ready for a meeting with some clients tomorrow." Her hair was wet, combed straight down her back and all her makeup had been removed.

"I clearly caught you at a bad time." Luke used his thumb to point to the door. "I can leave."

"Don't be silly." She pulled out a chair to indicate he should sit, and she sat down on the opposite chair. "You called today. Did you get the answer you were looking for?"

Luke placed his hat on the corner of the table and sat where directed. Charlotte handed him his cup. As she pulled her hand back she licked her thumb. "There was some caramel on the outside."

"I thought you were just being a tease." Luke blushed at his playful comment.

"Ha Ha. Very funny. So you didn't say. What did you want earlier today?"

A scoop of combined caramel and cream reached the entrance of her mouth. The spoon slid back out between her closed lips. He felt like moaning at the erotic thought in his mind. Choking and coughing, Luke worked to get his mind out of the gutter. "Earlier today, yes I called to just check in. You know, see if there was anything you might need. That I might be able to provide." He started shoveling ice cream into his mouth to stop himself from making a bigger ass.

"Oh, well, I think the house is coming along nicely. Unless you predict any delays or problems we are good to go." Charlotte placed her spoon inside the empty cup and set it aside.

"No, I don't predict anything going wrong. Look, can I be honest?"

"Of course."

"I called today just to talk. Not about work stuff." He placed his empty ice cream cup on the table and pushed it away. "I just wanted to see how your day was going."

"Oh."

"I should go." Luke went to stand when Charlotte placed her hand over his.

"Thank you." Charlotte looked directly into his eyes. "It's been a long time since someone, since a man has wanted to talk to me for me. I'm a lot out of practice picking up cues."

"Okay." He held her gaze.

"Okay." She squeezed his hand. "Can I get you anything else, water or coffee?"

"No, I'm good, but I should go. We both have early mornings. I just wanted to stop and give you the treat and check in on you, if that's all right?" He got up and this time she didn't try and stop him.

He walked toward the door and she followed. Luke turned toward Charlotte before opening the door. He leaned forward and kissed her on the forehead. "Have sweet dreams, Charlotte." He opened the door and left.

***

Stunned. He was the last thing she saw coming her way. She was completely and totally stunned that the t-shirt wearing, jeans hugging, southern cutie just shared ice cream with her and kissed her forehead. Charlotte thought at that very moment that if she knew what swooning was she could possibly do it.

She fell back against the wall. She stood, fanning herself with her hand, smiling like a fool.

Chapter Ten

IT WAS THERE. Sitting on the corner of her drafting table staring at her. Not really staring, it's a cell phone. Charlotte couldn't help it. She had been out of sorts and now this. Aimee had called and invited her over for dinner. She'd said she wanted to talk with Charlotte, and would have Derek grill out.

The idea of being out of the hotel for the evening was *very* appealing. The idea of being a third wheel, as Luke had referred to himself the other night, didn't thrill her.

Jessica walked in with a file. "I have those prices in here for the Gamboni's house."

"Thank you. Oh, and Jessica, I won't be taking your advice for dates anytime in the near future. Did you know your cousin had a very possessive girlfriend?"

Jessica covered her mouth with her hands and gasped. Then she laughed. "Oh gosh. No, I didn't know about a girlfriend. I need to go to more family functions. I guess there's a story?"

"There is a story. I'll explain some other time when I won't burst out laughing at how it looked when he was dragged away." They both laughed.

"Well, at least you're laughing about it," Jessica said. "This'll make for a fun family reunion story." She pointed to the file. "Let me know if you need anything else for that."

"Will do. Thanks. Oh, can you close the door?"

Jessica nodded and left Charlotte's office.

Before she knew it, Charlotte was calling Luke. "I wasn't going to call," she said. "But I didn't want to be a third wheel like you talked about, and I couldn't concentrate on my clients, and I hadn't even realized that I called when you answered …"

The background noise faded and a door slammed in the distance. "Good morning, Charlotte," Luke responded.

"Hi." She hadn't realized she was even capable of creating the breathy voice coming from her mouth. She cleared her throat. "Hi Luke. Funny thing happened a few minutes ago. You know my friend Aimee, the one you met? Well, she invited me over for dinner with her fiancé, and I thought I would ask if you had plans this evening. You know, so you could pay me back for helping you out the other night when you were a third wheel."

"Charlotte Cavanaugh, are you asking me out on a date?"

"NO," She shouted. Her palms were sweaty and heat worked its way up her body. "What I mean is, yes. I guess. Yes, no guessing involved. UGH." She leaned over her table and tapped her forehead on her latest floor plan. She rested her head on her arm and started the conversation over.

This is embarrassing.

"Luke Anderson, would you care to join me this evening for dinner at my friend's house?"

With a lightness in his voice, he accepted the invitation. "I would very much enjoy your company this evening. When should I pick you up?"

"Make it six?"

"I'll see you then."

Charlotte ended the call and texted Aimee. *I hope you don't mind. I'm bringing a date for dinner.*

***

Luke slapped Joe on the back. "I'm headed out. I'll see you in the morning."

"Are you meeting up with Charlotte? That's three nights in a row. Better watch out or you'll have a shackle on your leg like me." He laughed.

"If I'm ever so fortunate, we can be two deliriously happy fools together," Luke yelled over his shoulder as he closed the door.

Luke drove to Charlotte's hotel. He ran his hand over his cheek to make sure he hadn't missed a spot shaving after his shower. He realized his heart beat a little faster than normal at the thought of spending more time with her. He spent most of his time focused on building his reputation in the close-knit construction community. The idea of actively seeking out female companionship hadn't entered his mind. That Charlotte understood his daily grind was just another unexpected, pleasant factor in the complex equation of Luke's life.

Charlotte waited by the hotel's sliding doors under the portico. Luke parked and got out. As he walked around the front end of the truck, he couldn't help but smile. "Hi there."

"Hi. I hadn't told you where to meet me, so I just decided that since I was ready I'd come down to wait."

"I wasn't sure what to wear," Luke admitted. "Does that sound lame? I was stressing out like a middle school boy. Should I be telling you that?"

They both laughed. Luke helped Charlotte up into the high seat of his truck, then went around to the driver's seat. "Where to?"

"Oh gosh, I forgot you didn't know where to go," Charlotte said. "Head toward Dartmouth Street."

Luke proceeded in that direction.

"I have a confession," Charlotte said.

"Should I be nervous?" Luke glanced over at her as he turned a corner.

She gave him a shy smile. "I have four skirts, three pairs of jeans, two shirts, a sweatshirt and a jacket all piled on my bed."

They both laughed.

"How in the world can you have three pairs of jeans?" Luke said, still laughing.

"Well, I guess you don't have a sister. I was thinking I could go with skinny jeans and either my riding boots or heels. Then I have my boot-cut jeans with some fun sketcher boots. Then I was thinking of dressing ultra-slacker in straight-leg jeans and sneakers. A girl has many options."

"I guess so. Well, if it matters any, I like what you decided to wear." He took a chance to peek over at her to check

out her jeans-covered legs. He glanced up and saw her looking right at him.

She smiled. "The house is right over there."

Luke parked and walked around to help Charlotte down
from the truck seat.

"Aimee was surprised when I said I was bringing you
along," Charlotte said. "She did mention she wanted to talk
with me privately. Would you mind going outside when it's
time to grill?"

Luke stepped forward and reached for Charlotte's hand
to stop her before she knocked on the door. "That sounds
serious. Are you sure I should be here?"

"I don't know what she wants, but I'm sure it's okay. She
would have told me if something was wrong." She knocked.

Luke felt awkward, but the moment Aimee opened the door
with a warm smile, he relaxed. She leaned forward and kissed
Charlotte on the cheek. "Come in, you two. Luke, it's so nice to
see you again. I was pleasantly surprised when Charlotte said she
was going to bring someone along. Luke, I'd like to introduce you
to my fiancé, Derek. Derek, this is Luke Anderson. Luke and
Charlotte are working on a project together."

"Nice to meet you, Derek." They shook hands. The television was tuned to a baseball game, and Derek immediately
got Luke talking about the two teams playing.

"That's amazing. You get two guys in the same room
with a ball game on and BAM, instant conversation." Aimee
slapped her hands together.

Derek looked over. "Should I get the steaks on?" Aimee
nodded. "Okay, I already started the grill, so these babies
should cook up nice and quick."

Luke followed Derek out. "I'm sure you don't need help, but listening to Charlotte and Aimee talk girl talk might be too much for any man."

"Understood. They can complete each other's sentences. It's creepy, man, *creepy*."

***

Charlotte watched as Derek and Luke walked out the back door to the deck where she knew the gas grill was. She turned to Aimee. "Okay, spill. You said you had something you wanted to talk about."

Aimee moved closer to the corner of the oversized arm-chair and pulled up her knees. "The funny thing about life is that you can plan and plan, and yet sometimes things change. I prepare for work so when I walk into a courtroom I know exactly what I'm going to say and I'm ready for any situations that might arise. This is something I never saw coming. Derek is just as stunned, and the two of us are just looking for something normal. Something we would do any other night, which is why I asked you over and didn't balk when you said you were bringing someone."

"Aim, you aren't quite making sense. Do you have can-cer or something? You know you can count on me. I'll bring you to get treatments, whatever you need."

"How about diaper changes? Do you know how to do those?"

"Huh?" Charlotte was stumped. She heard the words her friend was saying, but it wasn't sinking in. This kind of con-versation hadn't come up at ANY of the times they'd met up for drinks. Charlotte and Aimee talked work. They talked about where they wanted their careers to go. They talked about getting married, but more about the fact that they wanted to be married. They'd never had a conversation about white picket fences, four and a half baths, a dog, and two-point-two kids. Charlotte knew the house she wanted; it was sitting in the woods, waiting for her to find all of its secrets, but she didn't need a husband to do that. Aimee and a baby. Aimee pregnant. This had never crossed her mind. Like a deflating balloon, she let out all her air and collapsed back into her chair. "Wow."

"Yeah, wow. Derek and I have been in a funk since we found out this morning. We thought that being engaged would make hearing news like this less of a situation and more of an event. Well, I think this situational event is putting my life on fast-forward. I don't know what I should do."

Silence hung in the air for what seemed like an eternity before Charlotte spoke. "You love Derek. I have no doubt about that. From where I sit, as your closest friend, you have two options. Option number one is to get married and have baby Charlotte, because you'll name your firstborn daughter after me and live happily ever after. Option number two is to give the baby up for adoption and still get married, and continue on with your life, on the timeline no one forced on you." Charlotte heard a noise from the kitchen, and looked over to see Luke looking her way. He tilted his head to indicate that Charlotte should follow him into the kitchen.

"Aimee, sit tight and think about what I said. I'll go check on the guys." When she got to the kitchen, she could see Luke was unhappy about something. "What's wrong?"

Luke moved closer to Charlotte so he could whisper in her ear. "I think I need to leave."

Charlotte leaned in to whisper back. "Are you not getting along with Derek? He's so laid back. I can't believe you wouldn't get along."

"It's not Derek. That guy out there is so happy he's getting married and having a baby. Then I come in here and overhear you telling your so-called best friend to put the baby up for adoption. I think you need to stay out of this."

Charlotte stepped back. "I don't think you fully understand what's going on."

"No, I don't know both sides of the story. But I do know it's not my place to be telling anyone what to do. This is for Derek and Aimee to decide."

Charlotte crossed her arms. "Really." Raising her eyebrows. "Listen, you don't know Aimee like I do. She's my best friend, and we've shared everything with each other. She brought this up because she wanted my opinion. You can't leave and make a scene. It will just upset Aimee. Please, just go outside. I'll explain more later."

Without saying a word, Luke grabbed the tongs and walked back outside. Charlotte watched him go, and she also knew in that moment things with Luke had changed.

She walked back into the living room.

"Anything wrong, Charlotte?"

Charlotte put a smile on her face. "Nope. Everything is fine. Luke just needed to find the tongs."

When the four of them sat down to eat, Derek and Aimee were their normal talkative selves. Charlotte felt the strain from her disagreement with Luke. He just didn't under-

stand how things were between her and Aimee. He shouldn't
have given his opinion. Throughout dinner Charlotte's an-
noyance with Luke grew. He acted like they hadn't even had a
disagreement.

After dinner was finished and while Aimee served up
strawberry shortcake for dessert, Derek suggested watching a
movie. Luke declined the offer.

"Sorry to cut the evening short, but I have an early day
tomorrow." Luke looked over at Charlotte. He tilted his head
and winked at Aimee. "I'm working on a house, and the designer is a slave driver."

Charlotte picked up her plate and walked toward the
kitchen saying under her breath, "You haven't seen slave
driver yet, Mr. Anderson."

Luke stood and Charlotte reached for the salad bowl as
they all helped clear the table. Aimee refused help with the
rest of the cleanup, so Luke and Charlotte made their way to
the front door. Derek gave Charlotte a kiss on the cheek and
shook Luke's hand. "Glad you could join us. It was nice to
have someone to talk to."

"It was good to meet you, Derek." Luke leaned over and
kissed Aimee on the cheek. "Aimee, take care."

Charlotte hugged Aimee, said goodbye, and headed to
Luke's truck. Luke reached the passenger door and opened it
for her. He helped her up into the seat, walked around, without saying a word. He got in the driver's side. Aimee and
Derek waited on their front step and waved as Luke drove
away.

The crunch of the tires rolling over the pebbles on the
road created a staccato, which echoed in Charlotte's mind.

They drove in silence all the way to the hotel. Luke pulled into the portico and stopped the truck.

"You don't need to help me out. I've got it." Charlotte reached for the door handle.

Luke lightly placed his hand on her left forearm. "I think we should talk."

"I think we've said enough to each other. You don't know the first thing about my relationship with Aimee to be telling me what to do or say."

"I'm sorry if I overstepped, but you're the one who brought me to that house. I won't hold my tongue if I see something out of place. It's not my style."

"You don't have to worry about that with me anymore. Thank you for driving this evening." Charlotte got out of the truck so fast Luke didn't have time to realize what she was doing.

"Wait ..." The truck door slammed and Charlotte walked quickly into the lobby of the hotel.

Chapter Eleven

THE PENCIL THAT had previously been behind Luke's ear flew across the room. The fuse on his temper was extremely short, and when he'd made a cut on the same piece of wood for the third time he thought he would explode. The sound from behind him by the door had him turn to see Joe walk in the library door. He greeted him in a clipped tone. "Hi."

"Well good morning, sunshine. Looks like you didn't get lucky last night."

"Shut it, Joe. I got here this morning to find a punch list waiting on my toolbox from Ms. Cavanaugh. It's a list of all the things that need changing."

Joe had the nerve to smile. "What the heck did you do, start a fight with her?"

Luke looked at the floor. When he looked up, he ran his hand threw his hair. "As a matter of fact, I did pick a fight with her."

Shaking his head, Joe leaned against a sawhorse. "What's your problem, man? Has it been that long since you've wooed a woman? Starting an argument will get you in the doghouse, not her pants."

"Didn't I say to shut it? I screwed up, but I just couldn't listen to her step into a situation she wasn't a part of. Her friend and fiancé have this thing, and Charlotte was offering her two cents. She needed to listen and then butt out."

"I don't think that's your place to say. Luke, man, you're new to this thing with her. Maybe she has that kind of relationship with her friend. Girls, well, they get a weird connection with other girls. Maybe that's what's going on."

Luke paced to the front windows and looked down on the dumpsters and porta-potty at the front of the construction site. Turning, he saw Joe watching him.

"You're right," Luke said. "This thing with Charlotte is new, and I don't know how things are between her and Aimee. I guess I should have asked her before getting on her case. But this …" He waved the punch list in the air. "This is out of line. She made this list and didn't include any change request forms. I need to verify these are actual changes and not just her being a bitch because we had a disagreement."

"You sound like a bickering married couple. Good luck. I'm going to finish up that molding and then I'm done here. If I'm done before you get back, I'll be heading over to that other job we've got going. I want to check on the crew over there before heading to that commercial project down on Main." Joe shook Luke's hand and left.

***

"Jessica, I need those files, like yesterday!" Charlotte yelled from her office. It was a busy morning; the phone had been ringing, and she was acting like a dictator. *What's come over me?*

"Knock, knock. I have those files you wanted. I just couldn't get them to you because of the phone." Jess came in.

Charlotte kept her head down like she was concentrating on her work. "Just put them on the corner. Thanks."

"Okay, also, um ..."

"Spit it out, Jess."

"Luke Anderson is here, and he has a punch list he wants to talk with you about."

At the mention of Luke's name, all pretending stopped. Charlotte looked up and saw the concern in Jessica's eyes.

"I can tell him you're too busy," she said. "Whatever you want."

"No, I need to clear that up with him. Please show him back."

"I know where your office is."

Charlotte stood at the sound of the low baritone of Luke's voice ... There he was, standing in her doorway. Black t-shirt stretched tightly across his muscular chest. The brown, well-worn belt rode low across his hips atop the equally well-worn jeans with the hole in the right knee. The frayed bottom of his jeans rested on top of those same dirty, scuffed up work boots. She really liked those boots. The sight of him made Charlotte's heart stop beating. She caught her breath, losing her train of thought.

Jessica cleared her throat. "I'll just, excuse me, I'll let you two just ... you know ... talk."

Luke stepped aside so Jessica could leave the room. Then he slowly closed the door with a quiet click.

"I didn't get to finish what I was going to say last night," he said. "I think we need to talk about what's going on between us, but that can be done on personal time." He spoke slowly and quietly. As he approached her desk, he looked at Charlotte like every word he said was meant to touch her heart. "Say you'll go out with me again tonight. Tell me you want to spend more time together. Tell me you want to figure out if we can be as good together as I think we can be."

"Yes." Charlotte's whispered answer resonated throughout the room, and when she spoke that one simple word she knew it was true. She did want to know more about Luke. To hell with waiting for the right time. Maybe the right time was now.

"Good. I do have some business to discuss with you, as well. Should we sit?"

"Of course, yes, have a seat." She waved her hand toward the empty seat. "Can I get you anything to drink? I have water, tea, coffee …"

"Nothing, but thank you. I found this punch list on my toolbox this morning. I admit I was rather … upset. A few of the things were on the schedule to be completed today. I double-checked them before I left to come over here. There're two major ones that would need to be put through with a change request."

"I apologize for the list. I should have consulted with you directly, but to be honest, after the way things ended last night, I didn't want to talk with you, and I wasn't sure if you

wanted to talk with me. I thought the list was the best solu-
tion. As for the two major ones, can I see the list?"

Luke handed it over. He leaned forward with his fore-
arms on the desktop. "It's these two I have highlighted."

"I'm sorry. I thought I made a note. I just need an estimate to show what that change will cost. I'm sure they won't
want it changed now, but I need to prove that it's cost-
prohibitive first."

"That's good. I'll get that back over to you by noon
tomorrow."

"Thank you. That'll work."

Luke reached out and held both of Charlotte's hands,
rubbing his thumb along the inside of her wrist. "This project
will come to an end. Your client will move into a very nice
home. You'll get involved in the next assignment. All that
being said, you and I don't have to be something fly-by-night.
I'll pick you up at seven. Wear jeans and bring a sweatshirt or
something. It might get cold." Luke stood, winked at a
stunned Charlotte and left her office.

Chapter Twelve

CHARLOTTE LEFT THE office at six after one of the craziest days. The phone hadn't stopped ringing, and she hadn't been able to focus on any one task she set for herself. Everything reminded her of Luke. Hints of cedar and orange scented her office. His scent. She felt as if he was there with her, holding her hand, gazing into her eyes. When she finally decided nothing was ever going to get done, she called it a day and told Jessica she would see her tomorrow. On the way back to the hotel, she decided to give Aimee a call. They hadn't talked, and Charlotte felt as if she needed to clear the air.

Aimee picked up right away.

"Hi Aims," Charlotte said. "I was hoping to talk with you for a minute."

"Hi Charlotte. I've been in and out of court all day, but I wanted to talk with you, too. Listen, I don't want this to sound short or ungrateful or that I don't appreciate you or our friendship, but when I told you last night that I was pregnant, I wasn't asking for advice. I just needed to unload. Derek and I have pretty much talked each other to death, and I was just looking for another body to unload all my nervousness on. You know I love you like a sister. Derek and I both love this baby so much already, but we're scared of the unknown. It's an unknown that you can't help with either. Any decision regarding the baby has to be made by both of us."

Tears blurred her vision. Tears of happiness. "Oh Aimee. That's why I was calling. I've been thinking about how things went last night. Luke said he thought I should've kept my nose out of your business and I got mad at him, which is why we left so early. But I kept thinking about what he said, and I realized I was wrong. I was wrong for dispensing advice when I had no right to, and wrong for snapping at Luke. I made a mess all the way around last night."

Aimee sniffled loudly over the phone line. "You know you aren't supposed to make pregnant women cry, right? If you were here, I'd hug you. I hope you spoke with Luke already. He is such a nice guy, Char."

"He is a nice guy, which is why I'm heading back to my room to change so we can go out tonight. We both have things to talk about, but first I need to apologize to him for my actions last night. I was a bitch when he dropped me off. At least he knows up front that I have a temper!"

They both laughed. "I'll talk to you soon," Charlotte said.

She parked in the hotel parking lot and headed for her room. Her cellphone rang just as she stepped off the elevator. She looked at the screen and cringed.

"Hi Grant. What can I do for you?"

"Hi Charlotte. I hadn't touched base with you in a while. I just wanted you to know that everything seems to be on time. If for some reason the schedule gets messed up, which I don't expect, I'll let you know if your installation needs to be changed."

"Thanks. I appreciate the information."

"You're welcome. I know I was upset when we last spoke. I'm just glad we can at least work together. Have a good night, Charlotte."

"You too, Grant."

To her complete surprise, they were able to end the conversation in a pleasant manner. Maybe things were turning around in a positive way. Charlotte's mood lightened for the first time all day, and seeing Luke again would be a perfect way to cap it off. Since he'd said to dress casually, she reached for a long-sleeve, downy soft, cotton t-shirt. The button on the relaxed fit jeans was a struggle, and she vowed this was the last night for eating too much. Charlotte tied her sneakers, found a sweatshirt and headed back down to the lobby.

***

As Luke pulled into the portico of the hotel, Charlotte walked out to meet him. He stopped the truck, and before he knew it she had opened the passenger door and jumped up into the cab.

"I decided to come down and wait. Those four walls were getting pretty boring to look at."

"I could have helped you up." Luke laughed at Charlotte's upbeat demeanor.

Charlotte flashed him a smile he hadn't seen until now. "I can handle getting into your pickup truck, cowboy."

"Cowboy! That's a new one on me." He laughed again. "Was that Becker leaving?"

"No, I just talked to him on the phone, though. We had a pleasant work-only conversation. Maybe things are going to smooth out after all."

"Huh, I could have sworn it was him leaving. Anyhow, I thought we'd have a picnic under the stars tonight. Nothing fancy." Luke put the truck into gear and headed toward the spot he had picked out for their evening.

He glanced at Charlotte. She was gazing out the window, enjoying the ride and humming along to the quiet sounds from the radio. He knew she realized where they were headed when she sat up a little straighter in her seat. "Are we heading to my house?"

"*Soon* to be your house is my guess, but yes. It has a great grassy yard with a large clearing for stargazing."

"My dog's going to love having all that space to run in after being cooped up in a kennel all this time."

"You have a dog? Why didn't I know this about you? He'll definitely enjoy all the space to run and the critters to chase. I hope you have a strong stomach. He'll most likely bring you some presents he catches."

"I'm not buying the house now, if it'll encourage my dog to start killing squirrels." The curve of her lips let him know she was kidding.

"Oh, you might enjoy it if he can keep field mice from living in your pantry. What's his name? What kind of dog is he?"

"If Sam keeps critters out of the house, I'm all for him being a hunter. He's a labradoodle, so I fear he'll be seeking out birds more than mice. He might decide a mouse is a good playmate, too. He's a lover not a fighter."

"Well, I can't wait to meet Sam and watch him run around with wild abandon." Luke flashed her one of those heart-stopping smiles that made her fan her red cheeks. She turned back toward the window.

The curve of her lips in the slightest of smiles let Luke know Charlotte was enjoying the drive. The last time she had walked through the house with him, she'd been excited and curious. Discovering all the house had to offer, through the eyes of someone new, made Luke long for days gone by. Yet, he was eager to see all that Charlotte could do with such a wonderful home.

This time, as they made their way in the truck up the long drive, Luke saw everything with a new perspective. Through the window, Luke was able to see the wonderfully shadowed landscape before him ... so many evergreens and tall, obviously very old maple and oak trees. Leaves covered the earthen floor from years upon years of seasonal change. The driveway showed a path from their previous visit only days ago, but everything else was undisturbed.

The house wasn't sold yet, and he was nostalgic for times gone by. His grandmother's apple pie, his mother's laughter and long forgotten walks along the hidden paths in between those giant trees.

Those same tall trees shielded the light from the low-hanging sun. Luke stopped the truck and they both sat for a moment, enjoying the serenity of their surroundings. "I love the sound of the crickets and the sight of fireflies blinking away. It brings me to such a calm state."

"Mr. Anderson, are you trying to woo me with Mother Nature? Because it just might be working."

They both laughed. "Come on," Luke said. They got out and he grabbed the picnic basket from the bed of the truck. "Can you reach the blankets from behind your seat? The grass might be a little damp this time of day."

Charlotte retrieved the blanket and they walked around to the side yard. That was when she pointed to the fire pit further off to the side. "Dinner by firelight? I hadn't noticed that before."

"I thought something like that would be nice. I confess I had help filling the basket. Stella came to my rescue after Joe went home and made fun of me for my ideas. She's a hoot. Reassures me there're still happily married people out there. You just have to be patient to find the right one."

"Amen to that. So, what can I help you with?" Charlotte unfolded one of the blankets and attempted to spread it on the ground by first flying it into the air.

Luke put down the basket and helped her spread the blanket out. They sat and he opened the top of the basket and removed some of the containers. "I also brought this." He pulled out a bottle of white wine.

"This is an adult picnic, so it wouldn't be complete without that. I can get our plates ready if you want to open it?"

She began filling their plates with fried chicken, biscuits and coleslaw. "All of this looks amazing. I needed some comfort food."

Charlotte took a sip from the glass of wine that Luke handed her. He watched as she licked her upper lip. He knew he was doomed when he leaned in toward her, reached his hand over and held her chin. He ran his thumb along her lips following where her tongue had been and then cleared his throat with a little shake of his head. "You had just a little, um, wine still on your lip."

Luke sat back and picked up his plate. His brain was buzzing with thoughts of how good it was to even be touching her. He was so lost in thought he didn't realize she had reached over and placed her hand on his arm.

"Luke, I can see the wheels turning, and you won't look at me. Please, look at me."

He did. Her posture said she was comfortable. Her smile subtle. In her eyes he also saw desire and hoped he wasn't wrong. "I have to confess that until lately, with you, I haven't spent much time alone with a woman."

"Well, I'm enjoying my companion and his choice of settings." She sat forward quickly and gave Luke a kiss on his cheek. "Now, let's finish this yummy food."

As the daylight slipped away and darkness descended, the cocoon that surrounded Luke and Charlotte seemed like the perfect shield from the distractions of everyday life. They talked about work, which they shared, and also revealed more about themselves beyond that they were both only children.

"It wasn't so bad being an only child. It hit hard when my dad passed at a young age, but my mom … my mom just passed." He took a moment to gather his emotions. "It wasn't unexpected. She had cancer. It's just, now that I'm alone, I'm not all that sure I could put a kid through that. You know? Losing a parent."

"I'm sorry about your mom, Luke. I didn't know."

Charlotte's arms wrapping around him was more comforting than Luke wanted to admit.

"I can't imagine having a baby now. My life is unsettled. But someday. My family was small, but I felt that love from my parents. I had myself fooled I had that kind of relationship before. Maybe that kind of thing can't exist in this day and age, but someday I'd still like to be a parent." Luke knew about Charlotte's relationship with Grant. What he didn't know was how disappointed she'd been about the loss of the house she'd dedicated herself to. "The house had been the focal point in our relationship. I realize now, once that was complete, so was our need to be together. Does that even make sense?"

"It does make sense." Luke stood and made his way to the fire pit. A small pile of split wood sat nearby, so he placed a few logs in the center of the ring along with a nest of small twigs, leaves and grass. "Stella thought of putting this in the basket, as well." He held up a candle lighter. He wasn't about to rub two sticks together to get a spark to start the fire. "No, I'm not about to use flint and steel." He was able to easily get a fire started making sure it wasn't going to escape the walls of the ring.

"The funny thing is I think my parents were more invested emotionally in my relationship than I was. I haven't told them yet." At the funny look Luke gave her, she laughed. "I know. A parent should know if their child is living in a hotel. I'm putting off having to face them. The disappointment I know I'll see in their eyes. They always wanted a big family, but it just didn't happen for them. I kind of grew up feeling the pressure was on me to make that happen. I do want a family. It will just be a little while longer till that happens. But I figured when I have the keys to this kingdom I can break all the news to them at once."

"It's funny that you're an adult hiding this from your folks, but I also think it's very sweet you're protecting them. My momma would've loved that about you. Not the keeping secrets, but that you love your parents so much."

"I think I would've enjoyed talking with your mom too. The woman who raised you had to be very special."

They put everything back into the basket except their glasses and the wine. Charlotte stretched her legs out on the blanket and leaned back on an elbow with her wine in the other hand, enjoying the scene with the fire and moon. "This is just a wonderful night."

Luke stretched out on the blanket, as well. "It is a great night." Looking up at the stars shining brightly above, he couldn't help but feel content in that moment. "This is nice. Sitting here, under the stars, relaxing next to a beautiful woman." He looked over at Charlotte, who had been watching him. "Too much?"

"Not at all, Mr. Anderson. As a matter of fact …" Charlotte moved closer to Luke, and he wrapped his arm around her as they lay back. She rested her head on his chest, listening to the beat of his heart. The feel of her hand as it glided up and down her back felt natural, as if he'd been doing just that for years. He thought alarm bells should be going off being this close to her, yet he was everything but alarmed. The glow and warmth of the fire protected them from the cool darkness that surrounded them. In that moment, Luke decided he needed to be even closer.

"Did you see that shooting star?" Luke asked.

She lifted her head to look at him. He had his eyes to the sky. "I wasn't able to pay attention to the sky," she said. "I was concentrating on the beating of your heart and the feel of your shirt in my hand. I was wondering if the feel of your skin on my fingers would be as reassuring as lying in your arms. You've wrapped me in a trance I don't want to snap out of."

"I think I like you in a trance." He brushed the back of his hand along her jaw. His fingers then ran through her hair. Looking into her eyes, as if drawing her into his protection. When his lips met hers, all reasonable thought escaped him, and his focus was on her and her alone, the softness of her lips, the smell of her perfume, and the hood of her sweatshirt, which at that moment seemed to be in his way.

Chapter Thirteen

HEAT RADIATED FROM his chest, surrounded him and he didn't want to let the feeling go. This was how he should wake every morning. Holding her till she awoke. Making sure she knew you were there for her. Not because you needed something from her, but just because you wanted to be with her.

Rays of sunlight started peeking through the trees on the opposite side of the yard and her breathing changed. He felt her tense up and she must have realized the heat on her back was Luke, cradling her. The weight of his arm over her side secured her to his chest. Like a cat relaxing, Charlotte began kneading the hairs on Luke's arm.

"Are you going to open your eyes to enjoy this sunrise with me?"

"I was just enjoying the feel of you holding me as I wake up."

Luke nuzzled his face into the hair at her neck. "I'm liking that, too. I was thinking I could take you to breakfast this morning. This makeshift bed is warm and all, but all night and all day on this ground, my back might start to protest, and I might not be able to walk tomorrow."

She laughed. "Fine, spoilsport." They dressed and Luke stood and started to fold the blanket that had covered them. Charlotte worked on the other blanket, which had been beneath them. He picked up the basket, put the blankets on top and held out his hand. Without any hesitation she held it, and they walked toward his truck.

"I just want to walk around the house, if that's all right," Charlotte said.

"Go ahead. I'll put this stuff down in the truck and catch up."

He found she had opened a side door to the house and was in the small library, looking at all the books. She turned at the sound of him entering the room.

"The door was unlocked. I guess someone was here recently and forgot to lock up."

"I'm sure since you're buying the house, it's okay to check things out."

She placed her hands on the back of the chair by the fireplace. "I've been meaning to apologize to you for my outburst the other night when we left Aimee's house. I should have spoken to you sooner."

Luke started to say something, but she interrupted. "No, let me finish. I talked with Aimee and she set me straight. When she told me she was pregnant, I assumed she wanted my opinion. I'm not used to someone not wanting my opinion. She reminded me that I didn't have a say in it. That was for her and Derek to decide. I felt like an ass. She knows I

love her, so she wasn't angry with me, but she wanted to remind me of my place and it's behind Derek."

"That's a hard realization."

"It was, for Aimee to have to say it and for me to hear it,
but it had to be done. I needed to be put in my place. I'm just
sorry I was too stubborn to listen when you said I needed to
mind my own business."

"I'm not sure about you, but I've gotten past that." Luke
walked over and wrapped his arms around her. He kissed the
top of her head. "So, since you're going to be the new owner
here, what do you envision for this place?"

Charlotte stepped away from Luke and started to look
around the room, running her hands along the bookshelves
and the backs of the chairs. "I see myself restoring this home
more than renovating it. I love the feel of this early American
style. I gravitate to this more so than modern styles. I've kept
my workspaces more eclectic because that's what people expect, but it's not necessarily what I like. It's a hard line to
straddle."

"I can imagine. I like that you want to restore this." Luke
noticed Charlotte had found the family bible. It was one of
the largest books in the room. She removed it from the shelf
and was opening the front cover revealing a family tree when
her cellphone chimed.

She looked at the phone and then at Luke. "Sorry, I
turned it on. It's a habit. I do it every morning." She closed
the book and answered the phone. She turned away from the
shelf toward the windows.

Luke looked at her and then at the book. The bible had
been in his family for generations. His mother had been the

last one to write in it. Why he hadn't bothered to look for it
he couldn't say, but he knew it needed to be with him and not
lost in the shuffle when they had to clean out the house after
it was sold.

Charlotte called his name. "Luke, I'm so sorry to cut our
morning short, but I need to get to the office. I have a cus-
tomer in Florida who's had something come up I need to
take care of right now."

"This is how life in our business goes. Let's head out.
I'm going to borrow some of these books."

"I'm sure no one will mind." Charlotte walked out of the
house ahead of him.

Luke carried a few books, the family bible being one of
them.

Chapter Fourteen

THE FLIGHT SOUTH to Florida went like clockwork. Even with a connection in Atlanta, Charlotte felt like it was a vacation rather than a work trip. Well, except her laptop, files and fabric samples, which served as a reassuring weight on her shoulder to remind her it was anything but a vacation.

The plane circled a wide arc around the light house at Ponce Inlet in a long and drawn out path. It landed at the Daytona Beach International Airport and Charlotte pointed her rental car east. Leaving the airport, she drove Richard Petty Boulevard to the long drive south down Clyde Morris with a median filled with palm trees. When she reached Dunlawton, she turned left, heading toward the Intracoastal and the Dunlawton Bridge. Over the side of the bridge, a manatee floated like a log while a dolphin raced along in the wake of a pleasure boat. From the time Charlotte was a child, she'd been coming to the Daytona Beach area, and she knew driving down Dunlawton was a more scenic route than taking International Speedway Boulevard to get beachside.

Traffic along the two-lane road of South Atlantic Avenue moved at a snail's pace with tourists unsure of where they wanted to go. Charlotte's mind was on everything that had to do with a tall, brown hair, brown-eyed southerner, and nothing at all to do with the house she needed to work at for the next few days. The brilliantly sunny day wasn't helping keep her mind on business either. Thoughts of sunscreen, towels and sea breezes were very tempting. She turned right on Beach Street, away from the ocean side of the peninsula toward the riverside and the quiet of Front Street.

The two story, white stucco house the Johnsons' called their Florida house sat among a lushly landscaped property. Pulling her car forward Charlotte noted that the landscaping was traditional Florida, with queen palms flanking the circular driveway. The lighting set in the ground to shine a spot on the trees at dark was a nice added touch. The St. Augustine sod had been laid, and the irrigation system was working as Charlotte drew the car to a stop.

The reason for the rush to the house was so that the Johnsons could leave for vacation, and the rest of their decor could be delivered and placed while they were away. According to the frantic call Charlotte received from Mrs. Johnson, *they just had to get away from it all.* The amount of billable hours Charlotte was adding to this project was obscene. She was just glad the Johnsons had already paid the majority owed. Getting stuck with a nonpaying client hadn't happened to her since she first started out in the design business. It was something she hated thinking about, and on emergency trips like this one, the thought was lurking in the back of her mind.

Charlotte grabbed her suitcase out of the car and used the code she was given to enter the house through the garage. The mudroom was home to the washer and dryer as well as a coatrack and bench seat. The coatrack currently held a beach bag and towels. She put her bag down on the bench and slipped off her shoes. She walked through the kitchen across the cool marble floor and into the living room. Her first task was to double-check the furniture that had already arrived against the file she had for the Johnsons' design concept.

The chirp of her cellphone could be heard, but Charlotte couldn't remember where she'd put it down, on the island in the kitchen or was it on the bench in the mudroom? She retraced her steps and found it blinking with three text messages from her office. She decided to just call back instead of trying to translate Jessica's shorthand texts.

"Cavanaugh Designs," Jessica answered.

"Hi there, it's me. Were you trying to get in touch?"

"Oh gosh, Charlotte. I didn't have a chance to talk with you. You obviously didn't check the weather before you left here. There's a hurricane headed right for Florida."

Mrs. Johnson had left bottles of water in the refrigerator and Charlotte reached in and grabbed one. "Okay. So, I probably have a week before it even makes landfall, if it even gets this far, right? I'll be back up north long before that ever happens." She headed back toward the family room to continue with her checklist.

"Charlotte, you're not listening. That hurricane is headed right for Central Florida, like tomorrow."

Charlotte stopped in front of the family room coffee table. "Let me turn on the television and see what their local weathermen are saying. You know how they love to blow things way out of proportion because they don't have anything else to talk about. I'll give you a call back once I know more."

Charlotte found a local television station out of Orlando and saw right away what Jessica was talking about. It was midday, and the television stations should have been showing a game show or soap opera, but instead the weatherman was pointing to a large, circular cloud that was spinning off the coast and would probably make landfall north of Fort Lauderdale. Evidently, the southern part of the state was already experiencing rain from the outer bands of Hurricane Linda. The winds were expected to pick up within the next few hours. Central Florida was predicted to start feeling the effects of the storm in the early morning hours. It was a category-two storm, but wind gusts could still cause damage and localized flooding was expected.

"On the bright side," Charlotte told herself, "the day after will be sunny, so cleaning up after Linda should be nice."

Just then her cellphone rang again. Luke. "Charlotte, I'm glad you picked up. I just saw the weather forecast for Florida. Are you going to evacuate?"

"Oh Luke, it's nice to hear your voice. I had no idea this storm was even out in the ocean when I told Mrs. Johnson I'd come make sure all her deliveries arrived on time. She's been a high-maintenance client, so I didn't think anything about coming down. Now I think it was just her wanting to get out of Dodge while this storm comes, and she wanted a house sitter."

"What do you have planned?"

"I just watched the local weatherman. I felt like he was downplaying it. He said it was a very compact storm, so the wind would be the worst. Not much flooding is expected. He also said something about taking the time to find my hurricane kit. I'm not sure what that is, so I guess I'll start looking in closets." She was walking from room to room, looking in closets for a box with an obvious *hurricane kit* marking on it.

"I have my laptop up. It says you should make sure you have gas in the car. A gallon of water for each person for at least three days. Is there food in the house? You should have food that won't need refrigeration just in case you lose power. Wait, are you in an evacuation zone?"

"Car is full, I just got it. There's a case of bottled water in the fridge. Hmm, not sure about the food. I'm pretty sure I'm in an evacuation zone. I wonder how I know if I'm supposed to leave? I should call the police or something."

"It says here this storm is only a category two. Not that that's not bad, but it could be worse. I was on the outer banks for a category two and lived to tell about it. The wind was the worst part, so if you can find someplace inside the house to get some sleep you should be fine."

Charlotte stood in the middle of the kitchen holding the phone to her ear with one hand and the other wrapped around her middle. The uncertainty was starting to make her nervous. "Thanks, Luke. I had no idea about this. I guess we live in a weather bubble until the winter. It's sunny or rainy, and then in the winter it's snowy. I usually just look out my window to see if I need an umbrella."

"You mean I can tell you there was a weather delay on the Sullivan's house?" He laughed.

"You are not delayed on the Sullivan house. Last I saw, you were all ahead of schedule."

"I saw that, too. I'm sure Mr. Becker is enjoying taking credit for that. I've split my guys between the house and the office complex we just started. Right now, it's good to be busy. So, tell me about this house you're currently stuck in."

"Well, it looks like every other house in Florida. Cinderblock and stucco with a coat of paint. Do you know Florida at all?"

"I've never lived there. Just went down for vacations. If this lady's got you working on putting some furniture in the place, it's way more than just a block house."

Charlotte looked around. "It is a stunning home. The back of the house faces west, looking right out onto the Intracoastal Waterway. They have an enormous boat parked right out back, an in-ground pool, a lanai with comfy chairs, and more varieties of palm plants and trees than I could guess."

"So that's the backyard. What's the inside like? Over the top?"

"Please, I picked out these furnishings. They are not over the top. Very traditional. No, not white-washed with palm tree fabric either."

"Now you just burst my bubble. I thought all Florida homes had the same look."

Charlotte laughed. Should couldn't help herself. Luke was a charmer and she liked it. "Okay, if you must know, there's a potted palm in the corner of the room right now."

"I don't believe you. There's no way the famous Charlotte Cavanaugh would put a potted palm in her design."

"Well, sometimes the client takes it upon herself to add things after I've finished decorating a room."

"Gasp. Say it isn't so." He laughed.

"You're so funny I almost forgot to laugh. Thanks, Luke, for distracting me."

"It is my pleasure."

Charlotte walked back into the kitchen and opened the pantry door to see what was inside. She sat down at the kitchen table still holding herself tightly, as if Luke were there with his arms wrapped around her. "So let me ask you something," she said. "What makes a Southern boy like you want to spend time with a bossy New England chick like me?"

"Wow, no pressure, right?"

"Seriously. You're a good-looking guy. It's late in the week. You could be out at a bar picking up any number of eligible young women, yet here you are talking with a woman who's hundreds and hundreds of miles away. Don't get me wrong, I wouldn't want you to be out trolling." She laughed nervously.

"The term trolling doesn't make me think about babes. Makes me think about my bass boat, which hasn't seen the water in a very long time. Spending time with you isn't a hardship, Charlotte. We have a relatively connected work life, which gives us common interests. Our personalities are compatible, and so far you don't seem like a bitch or an airhead like most of the women I've met since I've moved here."

"Now who's flattered? I'm not a bitch or an airhead. Listen, if Linda is coming to visit tomorrow I should get on the phone and figure out this delivery schedule. You know, just in case I do need to evacuate."

"That's a good plan. I'm only in Georgia, so if you need anything I can be there lickety-split."

"Georgia?"

"Just clearing up some family business. This lady friend of mine left town for work, so I decided it was a good time to leave town, too. All kidding aside, though, just call me if you need anything at all."

"You are so sweet. I'll be fine. I'll call you later. Oh, and good luck with your family stuff."

"Thanks. I'll be waiting by the phone."

He is such a goofball. The more Charlotte thought about him, Luke was becoming her goofball. That idea sounded pretty good, too.

Chapter Fifteen

ONCE STARTED, CHARLOTTE efficiently checked
off items on her to-do list. Several of the vendors delayed
their delivery schedules because of the impending storm. A
few vendors bumped their delivery time line up, so they were
no longer responsible for custom furniture pieces once
delivered.

Charlotte ate a sandwich over the kitchen sink, too ex-
hausted to sit down. When she finally sat on the couch, sleep
took over. The morning sunlight pierced her eyelids to rudely
awaken her. Maybe the hurricane turned out to sea. It doesn't
hurt to be positive.

Unfortunately, two seconds of watching the television
showed Charlotte she could kiss that sunshine goodbye later
in the day. While the system had stalled overnight, it had
picked up steam and headed north. Which meant Charlotte
had to get a move on if everything was to be finished before
the bad weather arrived.

Jessica emailed detailed flight information for later in the day. Charlotte felt confident she would be able to make that and return to the safety of her hotel home.

"Jess, I got the email. Thanks for getting that booked. I just have a few more things to do. Fingers crossed that all the deliveries arrive when they said they would."

"Did you talk to Luke Anderson?"

"Luke? I did yesterday. Why?"

"He wanted to know where exactly you were in Florida. I think he is worried about you."

"If the sun wasn't shining I'd be more worried about me, too. Listen, I need to go over my plans. If something comes up at the office you know how to get me."

"Will do, boss."

Jessica never failed to put a smile on Charlotte's face with her perky personality.

As if on fast forward, time had gotten away from Charlotte. One major delivery had arrived and been placed. She was waiting on one more truck to arrive and then she would be heading for the airport.

Picking up her buzzing phone she saw it was Luke calling. "Well hello stranger."

"It hasn't been that long since you saw me. Have you decided to find a surfer while you are down there?"

"Oh, I wish I had time for the beach. I haven't even gotten to see the ocean side. The river side is pretty out the back door, though." Then she looked out the back windows.

In the short time they'd been talking, the setting sun across the river highlighted the low gray clouds. The top of the king palms along the sea wall at the back of the property were moving steadily, and she noticed a constant ripple in the pool water.

"You got silent," Luke said. "Is something wrong?"

"Well, I don't think so. I just, well, I think maybe the storm is closer than I thought. The sun is hiding, the sky is gray, not orange or yellow." The lights flickered, went out, and then went back on. "Well, so much for that. The lights just went off and on. I guess electricity won't be reliable now."

"Maybe you should check your laptop for the latest on the storm. Do you know if the house has hurricane shutters?"

She opened her laptop, which had been hibernating since she finished working earlier in the day. "I've got the weather map up," she said. "It still appears to be offshore. I didn't notice any roll-down window covers when I drove up, but I vaguely remember the plans stating something about special glass? Is there such a thing?"

"You know, I have no idea. I don't build for that type …"

Charlotte's eyes were glued to the front of the house and she let out a bloodcurdling scream when she heard loud pounding.

"Charlotte? Charlotte, what's going on?"

"Oh God." She was shaking. "There was a huge noise and then I think someone just knocked on the door."

"Are you expecting a delivery? If someone was going to come and get you, I don't think they'd knock on the door." Luke heard rustling. "Are you shaking your head?"

"Yes, yes, of course it's a delivery. That's the whole reason I came down, to accept deliveries while they're gone." She slapped her forehead.

She reached for a small statue on the table by the front
door. She held the cellphone in one hand and the statue in
the other. "I'm going to open the door. I have a weapon in
case I need it."

"What's your weapon, in case I need to be a witness?"

"It's a statue of a shepherd boy." Charlotte turned the
statue over. "It's Lenox, so it should at least sting if I hit
someone with it."

"How about if you just answer the door."

"Oh, that's a great idea. I can hit him first. Get the advantage. Wait a minute. Are you laughing at me?"

"No, of course not. This is a very serious situation." He
laughed again. "How about you answer that door?"

"Jerk." But she laughed, too. "This is very serious. I
could get kidnapped."

She put the phone down with the speaker activated so
Luke could hear her. She opened the door a crack. Luke
stood holding his hands up.

"Luke? What the heck?"

"Don't beat me. Last night I couldn't sleep at all, so I
just got in my truck and drove. I needed to make sure you
were safe."

"Oh." All other words failed her. Charlotte flung herself
into Luke's open arms. Kissing his face then snuggling into
his neck. All the while squeezing him tighter and tighter.

"Easy there, killer. I can't be of any help if you squish the
air out of me."

"I am so surprised and thrilled." Kissing him some more.
"No one has ever done anything this nice for me."

"I'm sure they have. It was partially selfish on my part, too."

"Oh yeah, how so?"

"I'm going to catch some huge waves when the work is done."

"Come on in, goof, before all the air conditioning escapes the house."

Charlotte was good. Very good at what she did for a living. Luke showing up when he did would allow her some artistic freedom. He became the muscle for her relocating furniture plan.

"Since you arrived just as I was milling over some changes, you can help me move some things. What do you say?"

"I'm here to serve. As long as it gets us out of here and away from that hurricane faster."

Working side by side the rest of the afternoon exhilarated Charlotte. Equal partners, give and take, and something more. Subtle touches exchanged. A hand on top of the other. An arm around a back. Each movement, gesture, reminding the other that they were more than working partners.

The day progressed without word on the large delivery Charlotte expected. A steady rain started and wind blew the palm fronds. The sky to the south grew darker every time Charlotte stopped to look.

The chime of the doorbell surprised both Luke and Charlotte. She rushed to the door, but knew Luke wasn't far behind. The delivery driver huddled by the door to stay out of the weather.

"I'm so sorry it took me so long to answer the door," she told him. "Thank you. I hope you get back safely."

The delivery driver shook water off his head. "I'm going home now. It's getting crazy on the roads."

"Drive safe." Charlotte closed and locked the door. She placed the box on the table and picked up her phone. "I'm going to call to see if that flight north is still available."

She opened the travel information on her phone and clicked the link to the airline, which Jessica had included for her convenience. Charlotte and Luke walked to the kitchen. She hadn't realized Luke was carrying the box.

"Do you want to see what is in there?"

She was on hold with nothing better to do, so what the heck. "Sure, let's see why we waited all afternoon."

Luke cut the tape on the box with scissors he found in a drawer. Under scores of packing peanuts he found one delicate figurine. "This is what you waited all afternoon for?"

Charlotte couldn't believe her eyes. The figurine wasn't even something she had ordered. The deliveries she had expected never showed. By the look of the weather, they weren't going to arrive today either.

"I didn't even order that." She held up a finger. "Yes, hello. I have a flight scheduled to leave Daytona Beach and land in Atlanta. Can you check the status of that?"

"Why didn't you check on your phone?"

"I don't know. Jessica handles all my travel. It might have been faster, right? She answered Luke, and then she answered the airline representative. "The flight is cancelled? Like not even delayed? Okay, thank you."

"Looks like it's just you and me kid." Luke pulled Charlotte in for a bear hug.

**

"The wind is much worse than it was earlier. The delivery guy said I was his last drop-off. They called all the trucks back to their warehouses so the drivers could get home. I suppose I should start to get more organized about this storm stuff."

"Have you decided where we should hunker down?"

"While we were talking, when I first got here, I was walking around and saw a centrally located half bathroom. It has a sink and make-up counter to make it wide enough to stay in. I'll put some pillows in there with some water and granola bars I saw in the pantry. There is a weather radio in the laundry room we can get. I may be overreacting, but since I don't live here I'd rather be safe than sorry."

"If it helps any, I think your preparations are perfect. I for one want us to get back home safely."

They talked as they wandered the house, collecting what they wanted for their overnight stay in the small bathroom.

"I wish this bathroom had a bathtub," she said. "Then we could at least lie down."

"In a storm, most people think about putting the mattress on top of them for protection, not the comfort of lying on one."

"We have pillows, water and food, candles, *AND* matches, flashlight, weather radio and my charger for my phone. All we need now is a bottle of wine with a screw cap."

"No hot guy to finish off that list?"

"You fit the bill for that one."

"I was fishing for that compliment."

"I know." The lights blinked a few times and then went off. "DAMN." She did a quick walk-through of the house one way, and Luke went the other. Charlotte checked the television, but it wasn't working either. She decided she didn't want to be completely without communication, so she ran to the office. Grabbed her backpack and suitcase and brought them into the bathroom as well, just in case. It could be a long night.

Luke got cozy with a cushion under him and a pillow behind him. Charlotte sat between his legs leaning against him. "You never did tell me why you were in Georgia."

"I had a few things I needed to clear up from my mother's estate. It was just easier to do it in person."

"I'm sorry about your mom. I can't imagine what you have had to go through."

"It sucked. But meeting you, spending time with you has changed my perspective."

"How so?"

"My parents had a great relationship. I didn't think it could be duplicated. Then losing both of them left me. . . I don't know how to really explain it except to say I didn't want to get involved with anyone because I didn't want to feel that loss again."

Charlotte didn't know what else to do. Rubbing his arm comforted her. She hoped he felt some comfort as well. She hadn't expected to feel things for a man so soon after her breakup with Grant. She had been so sure that life would be fine alone.

Fireworks that exploded inside her head at the mere thought of Luke Anderson surprised her. It had been a very long time since she started a new romantic relationship. This surprise proved to be a pleasant one indeed.

"I understand where you're coming from. I convinced myself I didn't need anyone new in my life. I don't need you, Luke. Not like in a professional way. But I sure do want to explore more of what is going on with us. That is something I didn't expect when I moved into the hotel."

Sitting on the floor, in a bathroom, Luke's arms wrapped around her. The winds of a hurricane swirling around outside and Charlotte couldn't have felt more at peace.

Luke pushed the button on his phone and noted the time. "Eleven o'clock."

Charlotte played a few games on her phone and tried unsuccessfully to send a few text messages. Boredom set in and she got her nerve up.

She opened the door slightly to see if anything was wrong with the inside of the house. Nothing seemed to be amiss, so she stepped out of the bathroom followed by Luke. The back of the house was a wall of glass. "Look at how the wind is pulling the water out of the swimming pool." The palm trees had already lost much of the greenery at the top, and what was left moved violently from the force of the wind.

Luke stepped closer to the window just as a chair that had been positioned outside under the veranda flew by and smashed into a tree. Charlotte stepped back immediately watching the chair slide to the ground and tumble end-over-end until it was held in place by the garden wall separating the back yard spaces.

She walked to the door that led to the backyard. Charlotte unlocked and opened it so she could walk out to rescue the chair.

"What the hell are you doing?"

"Those chairs are expensive." She had helped the client pick out the outdoor furniture and knew just how expensive the chair was. Placing only one foot outside, the force of the wind pushed Charlotte against the doorframe. The wind hurt as it hit her, and Charlotte realized beach sand was hitting her.

Luke pulled her back in and locked the door. "Please, for the love of my sanity, don't go out there again."

"I won't argue with that. I guess we should just head back to our hole."

The lights flashed on, then off continuing to flicker, adding to Charlotte's increasing nervousness. Sleep eluded them both. Luke's strong arms held Charlotte anchored in their sanctuary.

At three o'clock in the morning Charlotte decided to look again at the backyard. The night sky was still black, and the rains were coming down, but the wind had diminished. The tightened muscles in her neck eased and Charlotte let out a slow breath. Exhaustion took over. She sat back down, leaning into Luke's arms. They slept the remainder of the night in the bathroom shelter.

**

Charlotte opened her eyes. The blue light from her cellphone caught on the mirror and illuminated the small space. She reached for the phone and saw the call was from Jessica. "Hi Jess, what's shaking?"

"I was going to ask how you were. How was the hurricane?"

"Hurricanes, they are so overrated," Charlotte said. They both laughed. "Really, I'm fine though. Luke drove down so I wouldn't be alone."

"Reeealllyy?"

"Funny. We stayed in the half bath all night. The phone woke me. What time is it?"

"Early, it's only six-thirty. I hate to have to tell you this, but Mrs. Camden called and left a message late last night. The police notified them that their new house had been vandalized. She said they were going over this morning to check out the damage. I know you need to finish up things there today before you head back, but I wanted you to know."

Charlotte rubbed her eyes as she cracked open the door and stepped out of the bathroom. She looked back to see Luke groan as he wiggled his shoulders. She made her way to the family room, inspecting for any signs of damage along the way. While she processed what Jessica was saying, she sat down on the couch. "I guess the first thing is to see how extensive the damage is at the Camdens. Stop over at the house to get a feel for the extent of the damage and send me a text. The insurance should cover any loss. This vandalizing messes up the timeline for the project more than anything. Please let

Mr. and Mrs. Camden know I'll be in touch and that I was in Florida at another client's house during the hurricane. I'll stop by myself as soon as I get back to town. I just need to accept two major deliveries today for this house, and then I'm coming back."

"All right, that sounds like a plan. I'll get on what I can, and we'll talk more when you get home. If something else comes up, I'll give you a call."

This day is going downhill, and it's only six-thirty. At least Luke is here to brighten things up.

Chapter Sixteen

WARMTH FROM THE sun beat down on the back of her neck as Charlotte bent to scratch Sam under his ears. Walking him around the park helped clear her mind, get centered. Reflecting back on recent events confirmed that things were looking up for the first time in weeks.

The work trip to Florida had been the trip from hell for Charlotte. It just wouldn't ever end. The deliveries had arrived a day late, after several phone calls to confirm there was someone at the house to accept them. Once the storm had passed she insisted Luke head home. He had his own business to take care of. Then she had trouble getting a return flight north due to all the flight cancellations up and down the eastern seaboard. In reality, Charlotte had never expected to be so happy to see her hotel room home.

Dinner with her parents the first night home had also turned into a pleasant surprise. Both were stunned by her breakup with Grant. Guilt in not confiding in them sooner weighed heavily on her. Charlotte realized that accepting her parents help wasn't a sign of weakness. She wouldn't stay with them, but she would be grateful if they would keep Sam for a while.

"Of course, we will gladly watch our grand fur baby." Charlotte's father was a sucker for Sam.

With her parents on board with dog sitting, Charlotte called the kennel so she could spring Sam from his temporary home. At least she knew he was going to be spoiled rotten. No guilt.

She had dropped her suitcase to the floor and collapsed onto her bed. Charlotte lifted her cellphone and saw she had several unread text messages. Standing, she stretched her arms and headed right back out. The first stop was picking up her puppy, Sam. She decided she needed to spend some time with her pup, so she leashed him up and walked across the street to the park. She was on the far side of the park when her cellphone buzzed. It was her mom.

"Hi Mom."

"Charlotte, are you out walking your dog at the park?"

"Yes, are you stalking me?" They both laughed.

"Funny Charlotte. I'm in the car and I just drove by. Stay there. Do you have a minute?"

"I was going to bring Sam to you."

Her mother parked and got out of her BMW. She greeted her with a kiss on the cheek and her mother crouched down to greet Sam, who was dancing around their legs.

"He is a cute dog. Your father is going to be so happy to have a companion to walk with."

"It means a lot that you'll have him. There have been a few things that I have felt guilty about and Sam not with me was one of them."

"We're happy to help. How long do you think you'll be in the hotel?"

"Well, I'm looking for a new house, so fingers crossed it won't be long." Charlotte felt slightly embarrassed at the situation. Not because of her breakup, but for feeling like she had failed her parents in some way. They had been making hints about 'getting older and still without any grandchildren.' It was a lot of pressure to be under for an only child.

"Oh Charlotte, you know your father and I are more than happy to have you come home till you get settled some-place else." Her mother hugged her.

"I know, Mom. It just feels like cheating if I run home to you. I'm a grownup. I should be able to manage. I can run my own company, but somehow my personal life is a disaster."

"It's not cheating to accept the help of family."

"I know and thanks for helping with Sam, Mom." Charlotte hugged her mother. She crouched down to give Sam some attention. "I guess deep down I didn't want to dis-appoint you. Quite the setback on getting grandchildren." She looked at the ground and then back into her mother's eyes and stood. "But I have to confess. I did want to do this on my own, too. I found a great house, so I was going to tell you everything after I moved in. I just know how much you were wishing for a ring and all that."

"Your father and I only want to see you happy, honey. I can't wait to see the new house you've picked out."

"I'm excited about this house, too. It's old and loved, and I can tell there are lots of stories. The thought of restoring it gives me goosebumps. I don't get that kind of opportunity with all the new houses I work on, so this is extra special because it's just for me."

"Oh Charlotte, you look happy. I can't wait to share the news with your dad. There is a reason for everything. Take one day at a time."

"It's all I can do."

"I hate to run, but I have an appointment I need to get to. Drop Sam off with your dad. I love you, honey."

"Love you too, Mom. And thanks for your support." They hugged and Charlotte watched as her mother got in the car and drove off. "Well, Sam, looks like your grandparents get to keep you for a little bit. Let's go, guy. I need to get to work so I can pay for your new playground."

Vibrating and buzzing alerted Charlotte to an incoming text message. Seeing Grant's name on the screen soured her happy mood. She hit the lock button and put the phone back into her pocket. Reaching down she rubbed Sam's neck as they walked around the park and to her car. Things were starting to work out, and she didn't want anything to spoil it. Especially Grant.

Sam excitedly ran into her father's waiting arms when she dropped him off for his vacation. "Don't spoil him!" Laughter followed her back into her car. She knew her dog was going to be fat and happy when she brought him to his new house.

It's a good thing he will have lots of room to run.

Charlotte pulled into the parking lot and made her way to work. Everything looked in order as she went into her office waiting room. Jessica was talking on the phone, so she waved and proceeded back to her private office. She was sorting through some of the file updates Jessica had left for her when she heard a knock on the door. It was Jessica.

"Hi Charlotte. Glad you finally came back from paradise."

"I have to admit, I never thought I'd be so happy to get out of Florida. Going on vacation is one thing. Being trapped there with no end in sight is a completely different story. So, hit me with the most urgent things."

"Since we last talked, things are going as planned. Mrs. Camden said the insurance company was going out there this morning, so they should know more shortly. I checked things out, and honestly, it didn't look that bad. Maybe a few hundred dollars to fix the damage. I think she's just freaking out because, let's face it, her home was invaded."

"I can sympathize with that. I'm going to swing by there while I make my rounds checking out the progress on the other houses. Anything new I need to look into?"

Jessica looked down at her notebook. "Yes, I have a few new potential client meetings set up for next week. They all understood when I put them off for a few days because you were stuck in Florida. It's great to have them at least start off understanding."

"All right. Let me go over these file updates. I'll head out in a minute. I'd like you to check on some orders. I'll give you the information when I leave."

"Charlotte, one more thing. Grant Becker called. He said to remind you about going with him to the gala at the library."

"Ugh." Fumbling the items in her hands, Charlotte couldn't believe the timing. "Yes, I did forget."

"Sorry to be the one to tell you. As for the other things, I'm pulling those fabric samples now. In case you want to take them with you."

"Thanks."

Jessica left Charlotte's office, closing the door behind her. After a few minutes of catching up with the workload, she felt comfortable with how things were proceeding with her clients' projects. With a sigh of relief that her career hadn't gone in the dumpster while she was off the grid for a few days, she relaxed and picked up her cellphone. She scrolled down her contact list and found Luke Anderson. He was the one she wanted to call, but she needed to respond to Grant.

Reading Grant's previous text reminding her of the event that evening, Charlotte typed her reply: *Of course I remembered. I'll meet you there.*

The limo is already arranged. I will be there to pick you up at seven. At least Charlotte could be grateful he hadn't been long winded. Hopefully, the evening wouldn't be long either.

Deciding not to let her impending evening with Grant bring her down, Charlotte tried to call Luke. Once, twice, three times she got voicemail. "Hi, I guess I'll leave a message since you'll see I called. So, I guess I was just saying I am finally back in town. I didn't know if you had time to get together and catch up." The phone stopped recording. *Damn.*

She hit the redial button. When voicemail clicked on again, she continued her message. "I hate these things. Worst invention ever. Anyhow, just give me a call when you get a minute." She sounded needy, or clingy. *Weird.*

Chapter Seventeen

PEERING OUT THE lobby doors, Charlotte swallowed down a sour taste and her stomach rolled. Attending this event next to Grant was the last thing she wanted to do. Keeping up appearances for her business, in front of the business community, kept her from calling and backing out at the last minute. The last minute past, time was up; the limousine pulled into the hotel portico precisely at seven. Deciding that attending this function was part of the job, Charlotte placed a smile on her face. The Screen Actors Guild should have been notified of the performance she knew was about to happen. Then again, this wasn't about her or Grant. This was purely about raising money to help the library modernize their outdated facility.

The event greeter at the library door checked them in and directed them to their assigned table. Waving, shaking hands, smiling, saying hello. Charlotte felt like she was at a political event rather than a library fundraiser.

Standing next to Grant with nothing to say was pathetic. Charlotte turned her head to the right, then the left. Spotting what she looked for, she moved. "I'm getting a glass of wine." Without even looking back, she started to walk away from Grant. Hairs on the back of her neck raised in alarm as his cold hand clamped onto her elbow.

"You will act cordial with me, Charlotte. Appearances are of the utmost importance. I can't imagine that you want potential customers to witness any unpleasantness between us."

Smile plastered on her face, she stared daggers at Grant. "Get your hand off me, Grant." He did as he was told. "Now, since you are here, I would like a glass of merlot." He inclined his head and stepped forward to place their drink order. It was then, as she scanned the room, that she felt him.

He stood across the room, focused on her. Several men gathered around him talking, laughing. They had no idea he wasn't looking at them, just her. Heat radiated from her core. Luke's intensity and utter focus on her nearly had her begging him from across the room for his touch.

"Charlotte, the emcee said we should go back to our table." Grant spoke right next to her, but his words were lost to the loud beating of her heart.

"Charlotte, let's go."

She obeyed Grant's directive. Charlotte knew that she was headed in the right direction. Toward Luke.

He walked toward the table next to hers. It would have been too good to be true if she was seated next to him. *Was it possible he hadn't really been looking at me?* She secured her hair

behind her ear, then did it again. Self-doubt crept into her
thoughts. Unsure of herself or how things stood with Luke
put her in a position she hadn't been in before. She had previously been wrong about men, especially the one seated next
to her. Luke could be upset with Grant's presence at her side.
She needed to explain.

Pleasantries were exchanged with the rest of the guests at
her table. Dinner was served and then cleared. All the standard actions performed, and yet all of Charlotte's senses focused on one single man sitting at another table. The cut of
his suit coat had been precise. He hadn't rented the tuxedo.
Luke Anderson was a man of surprises, and Charlotte wanted
to know more.

Approaching the podium, the president of the library
gained the attention of everyone gathered. "Before the live
auction starts, I wanted to take the opportunity to thank a
few of our event sponsors. Charlotte Cavanaugh Designs,
Grant Becker Construction and Luke Anderson Custom
Carpentry are the generous gold sponsors."

An echo of Luke's name being mentioned in recognition
with her own bounced around the room. Or was it just in her
head? Turning, looking, finding him, flashed a round of
butterflies in her tummy. A mere moment of eye contact
stirred desire in Charlotte that had never been present with
the man escorting her tonight.

"If you'll excuse me. I'll be right back." Charlotte didn't
wait for Grant to say anything. To his credit, though, he did
stand as she left the table.

Thankfully, the ladies room was empty. Charlotte went
in the room knowing it was one of the few places Grant

couldn't follow her. Luke's eyes on her for even a moment drove her crazy with desire to be next to him, to be his date for the evening. Acid burned her throat as the need to end this event's charade with Grant rose up. She might have arrived with him. She might be attending with him, but she was no longer in a relationship with Grant Becker.

The long skirt of her dress brushed her legs as her long stride carried her back toward the main hall to end this farce. Charlotte focused on the double doors, almost missing Luke's relaxed pose leaning on the wall. *Almost.*

"Are you in a hurry?"

"Oh!" Her hand went to her mouth to stifle a screech. "You surprised me. In a very good way I assure you." The exchange of smiles between them could have been interpreted by a witness as nothing but pleasantries. Charlotte clasped her hands to restrain them from sliding along his clean shaven cheek. "You shaved."

"I thought it was a good idea."

The electricity Charlotte felt bouncing between them was much, much more.

The door opened and Grant walked out. "Charlotte, there you are. There is a couple inside looking for you."

His dimple shown, telling her with his smile, Luke knew the inside joke that had just been spoken.

"Go."

"It's just business." She spontaneously laughed at her stuttered statement.

"I know. You should go back to meet with those people."

"Thank you." Walking away from Luke was the last thing she wanted to do. She refused to think of it as walking toward

Grant. Instead, Charlotte walked past Grant with enough distance so he couldn't touch her. "Can you point out who it was that asked to speak with me?"

Genuine surprise flashed across Grant's face. "Who? Oh, the couple. Hmm, I can't seem to find them." Speaking louder than before, "The auction is over, we should dance."

Several heads turned their direction. Creating a spectacle was not Charlotte's idea of fun even though embarrassing Grant would be fun. Grudgingly, she went toward the parquet dancefloor. Hand in hand, Grant pulled Charlotte closer. "This is a great song."

"This will be the last time I dance with you." The conversation was over. As far as Charlotte was concerned, the evening was over. She had made her appearance. Her business contacts would be appeased by her supportive donation. Leaving was the next phase.

"May I cut in?" His soothing Southern accent released a wave of nervous energy. Locking eyes with Luke, Charlotte knew that question was more a statement of his intent.

Removing her hand from Grant's grasp, Charlotte stepped away from him. "Of course you can cut in." Turning her back on the past, she faced her present, or could it be her future.

Music surrounded them and other couples moved around. The magic bubble Charlotte envisioned Luke joining her in shut out all the other nonsense of the night. Just the two of them moved, body to body. His woodsy scent woke her dormant spirit.

"I'm glad you came tonight."

The comment took her by surprise. "Really, I had regretted coming. That is, I did until I saw you across the room."

Her hand in his hand. His hands at her back guiding her around the dance floor. Moving as one. *This is the way it should feel.* Her inner voice surprised her. This moment, with Luke holding her, felt right. She didn't need to be with him; she wanted to be with him.

***

The moment he spotted her the evening had become a game. No, not a game, a mission. Luke focused on getting her in his arms. The dance floor proved to be the perfect opportunity to hold Charlotte close. Leaving her in Florida was one of the hardest decisions he had recently made. He wasn't looking for a relationship, but this was better than *nice*.

"I was surprised you showed up with Becker after everything that went on between the two of you."

"Trust me, arriving at this shindig with him was not my idea of fun. We had prearranged to sponsor a table. Three months ago I didn't know he was a lying cheating bastard."

"I can see where that might make you second guess a decision to attend an event with someone." The cheeky comment was meant to put Charlotte at ease. The smile on her face let him know he was successful.

The music slowed as the orchestra transitioned into the next song. Charlotte's right hand perfectly secure in Luke's larger callused hand. The weight of her left arm above his right arm allowed Luke the pleasure of gathering her even closer. Spreading his fingers across the satiny material of her back revealed the surprise of her bare lower back.

The quick intake of her breath let Luke know Charlotte was just as surprised by his touch.

Turning in time to the music. Their bodies held tight together. Luke's lips brushed Charlotte's ear. "I think I like this dress."

"I think I like the way you make me feel while I'm wearing this dress." The hushed words reminded Luke of their place on the dance floor, among the crowd.

The conductor turned toward the room giving a much needed pause in the musical selection. Charlotte's hand still in his, they made their way to the edge of the dance floor. Spotting Grant, Luke made his decision. "Charlotte, can I escort you home this evening?"

"I thought you'd never ask." This time she took the lead, holding tight to his hand. Grant stood holding her handbag. "Thank you for holding my bag Grant. I'll see you."

Without waiting for his reply Charlotte walked past, still holding tight to Luke's hand. He couldn't help it. He winked at Grant. The poor sap was so stunned by her quick actions he stood with his mouth gaping open.

Chapter Eighteen

SHE GATHERED THE files she needed to take with her for the day and put them into her backpack. Events from the past evening flashed like pictures in her mind. Finding him among the crowd. Dancing. Leaving together. Waking up in each other's arms. Charlotte was convinced that she had a better time than Cinderella had at her ball. Luke was her Prince Charming. She hadn't been looking for him, but he sure made her feel worthy of a crown.

Shaking off the euphoria might be near to impossible, but the list on the edge of her desk slapped reality into place. Picking up the rest of the files, she carried them to Jessica's desk. "These are the things I need you to work on." She saw the pile on the edge of the desk for her. "Oh, the fabric samples, great. Thanks for organizing that. Call if you need me."

"Will do. Oh, I sent a text to you a while ago with those new client appointments I made for next week, so you can put them in your phone."

"Thanks Jessica, I did see a few unread texts before I got here. I'll get them noted." She waved as she walked out of the office door.

Charlotte decided that her first stop for the day would be her new home. While in Florida, she'd gotten a call from her realtor, confirming that her offer to purchase the home had been accepted. All of her financing was taken care of, so the closing would happen within the month. She knew with a house that old there could be a holdup with the title work, but her end of this deal was done. She just couldn't stay away, though. Today she wanted to plan out any landscaping changes. There were some flowering bushes she'd thought of removing, but most of the flowerbeds would stay. It just needed to be cleaned up.

Beams of sunlight pierced the canopy of leaves. Charlotte lowered her car window as she approached the house. The crunch of the dried leaves under the tires reminded her of how little this house had been visited. It made her even more curious to know who had lived there. How could they have left such a magical place?

She stopped the car and gazed out at the property, admiring how well it had been cared for. Considering the number of trees surrounding the area, one would think there would be piles of leaves collecting along the house, under the bushes, and yet there weren't. That was great news for her, but it made her more inquisitive. She wondered if she would meet this caretaker when she signed for the house at the closing.

Charlotte searched and found the text message with the lock box code. To her surprise, when she reached for the door handle, it turned and opened before she'd even inserted the key.

Cautiously, she entered the house, holding the key and her phone like weapons. She wasn't sure what she was planning on doing if she found intruders, but at least she could throw things at them.

Charlotte's movements froze as scraping sound of a chair being dragged across the floor gave away the burglar's presence. Biting her lip to contain her nervousness, she followed the noise, and to her surprise a man in the library was quite cheerily removing books from the shelves and placing them in boxes.

"Hello?" Charlotte knocked on the door.

Luke turned around with a wide smile. He put down the books he held and approached her.

"Hi, this is a great surprise to see you. I didn't plan on seeing you today." He walked to her and kissed her on the cheek.

Stunned, Charlotte couldn't put words to the questions in her head. "Luke? What, how … what are you doing here?"

Luke held her hand and kissed her again. "I wanted to surprise you. This place needs a lot of work, so I thought I would help with packing up some of the stuff that was on the shelves."

Charlotte moved over to the far wall to look at the books and knick-knacks. "That's nice of you, but I can pack up things that are left behind."

He returned to the shelves and continued removing things, despite her comment. "It's no problem. I had the extra time." He looked over to her.

"Luke, please stop what you're doing. I want to go through all the things. I want to learn about this house before I can make any improvements."

"Just let me finish. I'm almost done."

"Just stop." She spun to face him. Dust motes floated in the air between them in a haze. He was just another example of a man trying to tell Charlotte how she was going to live her life. Controlling her. She thought he was different. This house was hers. He couldn't take that from her. Not again. She wasn't going to let another man tell her how she could live her life. This time when her dream home was completed, there wouldn't be a person alive that could tell her she had to move. This was going to be her house.

"I'm sorry." He closed the box and lifted it. "I guess I'm just used to helping out. I'll put this in my truck and be out of your way." Luke moved to walk around her. "Can I say something? My father passed a while back and it was just me and my mom. I liked that she had to call on me to help her. I hadn't ever been needed by another person like that. I know you don't need me like that. You've proven that with your business. It's just I would hope that there would come a time when you would just like it if I helped. Even with the small stuff. You know, just to know that I'm around."

"I do like having you around. But this ..." Charlotte waved her hands indicating the room. "This is going to be my house. I've made a grave error in asking for so much of your help. I've led you on, and I honestly didn't mean to. I cannot start another relationship. I need to settle my life, my personal life."

"I knew from your expression the first time you stepped foot in here. You appreciated every nook and cranny, from the built-in with the sticky latch to the busted sconces in the hall you said should be refurbished. I knew you'd modernize the mechanicals and make the house safer, but you'd keep the integrity. I knew because you let me see this house through your eyes. You let me in, Charlotte. Don't be afraid of that. I want to see your vision for the future come true."

"I appreciate your trust in me. But I think you're wrong. I think my vision is of only me. I hope you can respect that." She started toward the door.

"Charlotte, please wait." She turned. Luke walked toward her, but stopped short when he saw the crease in her brow and the sadness in her eyes. "Charlotte, I know this is right."

She just nodded. The lump in her throat was making it even harder to breath. When she reached her car and started it up, she was startled to feel tears running down her cheeks. She was getting her dream home. Her life was coming back together. And yet, that conversation with Luke had left her feeling empty. Seeing him in the library felt right. Like he should've been waiting there for her, but instead what she saw was him taking over and making decisions for her. She let Grant do that, and in the end it led to bitter disappointment.

Chapter Nineteen

CHARLOTTE PARKED THE car in front of the Camden's house. She wanted to focus on work, not her personal life, so she decided to check the fire damage to see how extensive it was. Mr. Camden had expressed a concern for the budget, and planning for changes on the interior details might need to be considered. She grabbed a notepad and pencil as well as a tape measure and headed for the house.

She used the key she had to enter the front door. A noticeable absence of hammers pounding and saws buzzing highlighted the extreme quiet. Charlotte's own footsteps echoed on the wood floor as she walked through the foyer and into the living room. Nothing appeared to be damaged. She secured the tape measure on the wooden trim to measure the front window. Curtain fabric had been approved, so she would need to sit with Mrs. Camden to decide on a style and hardware next for the windows. Those are some of the things that could save them money down the line.

Charlotte walked to the back of the house to inspect the family room next. The drywall damage was limited to the exterior wall between two windows. She measured the space that needed to be repaired and noted the dimensions on the notepad. In her estimate, it was a minor setback. Using her cellphone she took a picture contemplating how cruel it was to do such a thing to a nice family. Charlotte gathered her things and moved on.

She entered the kitchen next. Crashing glass brought Charlotte's attention to the side of the room. Glass shattered and fell all around. Out the window, a silver Lexus drove off. Seconds ticked by before she realized that a fire was spreading out across the floor. Flames licked at the bottom of the cabinet doors. Black smoke danced higher and higher filling the room. Candle stick holders that were intended for decorating the room stood on the counter waiting for Charlotte to place them in a permanent spot. Charlotte picked the largest one up and threw it, smashing the glass door leading out of the house toward the patio. Running toward her escape she passed a fire extinguisher. Sliding to a stop, Charlotte grabbed the canister and began to spray as she walked around the island. Flames continued to climb their way up the curtains framing the shattered glass of the door. Steadily working her way back to the interior of the house, Charlotte continued spraying the flames.

Coughing and choking, the smoke caught in her throat. Swallowing proved to be a painful task. She spun, turning around in both directions to find the next spot to extinguish. The flames were out. Without even thinking she pulled her cellphone from her pocket and called in the emergency. She relayed the address and that the fire was out.

Blinking away tears that continued to stream down her soot-covered face, Charlotte found her way back to the front of the house and sat on the front step. Sirens wailed in the distance. The reality of what just happened still hadn't sunk in. Sitting, staring off into the yard, struggling to calm herself, Charlotte waited for the firetruck. They would know what she needed to do, because right then, Charlotte had no idea why her entire body was shaking.

***

Once the last box was packed, Luke loaded it into the back of his truck parked near the back door of the house. His cellphone chimed with Joe's ringtone.

"Hey Joe, what's up?"

"Luke, man, I just got wind that the Camden house was ransacked and then firebombed."

"What?"

"That's not the worst of it, either. Charlotte was in the house inspecting the damage from the break-in when the fire started."

"What?" Luke slammed his truck door shut and started the engine. Frantic, he had to get to her. He had to make sure she was all right.

"She's fine, from what I heard. I guess she was able to tell the cops the kind of car that drove off, and she even put out the fire herself."

At the end of the driveway Luke paused before pulling out onto the country road that led back toward town and the subdivision where the Camden's house sat. He blew out a deep breath. "She's all right?"

"I'm not there, but I heard she is. You should check up on her. See for yourself."

"I'm already on my way there." Luke hung up and pulled out onto the road. He had to see her for himself. She'd left just a short while ago, and he knew she was upset with him. If anything had happened before he had been able to resolve things with her, he wouldn't be able to forgive himself. He mentally kicked himself for not being upfront with her about owning the house. He should have done it right away. Then again, they might not have gotten so close. He might not have gotten to know her—the real her, with the hopes and dreams she had.

From the entrance road to the subdivision, Luke could see the plume of gray smoke. It wasn't black like an ongoing fire, but like a fire that was smoldering. Police cars and fire-trucks blocked the road. He pulled over and parked. A few yards away, an ambulance with its doors open sat angled at the curb. He headed in that direction to find Charlotte.

A voice from behind caught his attention. "Sir, you can't be over here. I'm going to have to ask you to leave."

He turned. "I'm looking for Charlotte Cavanaugh. I was told she was in that fire."

"Who are you?"

"Me, I'm—" he hesitated. "I'm her fiancé. Luke Anderson. Charlotte is the interior designer who was working on that house."

"Come with me, Mr. Anderson."

Luke followed the officer to the back of the ambulance. Charlotte sat on the end of a gurney inside. She didn't notice Luke at first, so he had time to look her over, to make sure she was in one piece. He saw her hands tremble as she pushed her unusually messy hair from her face. A streak of black ran across her cheek. "Charlotte."

"Oh Luke." Tears rolled down her cheeks. He stepped up to get closer and she leaned over. Wrapping her in his arms, he held her. She probably didn't realize she was comforting him as much as he was trying to comfort her. He'd had no idea the extent of the danger she'd been in. Any harm to her would have been too much.

Luke leaned back, looking in her eyes. "You're okay?" He wiped at her cheek to try and remove the black marks.

"I'm okay. Freaking out, but I'm okay."

"Ms. Cavanaugh?" They turned at the sound of her name being called.

"Yes." Luke stepped aside so the officer could talk with Charlotte.

"I just wanted to say that you can go home now. We have your contact information, so if anything else comes up we'll call. Do you need a ride home?"

"I'll bring her home." She was his. Possession came from deep within Luke, which he hadn't used before. Wide eyed, she quickly looked up at him. "That is, if you want me to," he added, looking down at her.

"Thank you, officer," she said. "I'm being taken care of."

"Sir, may I have a word with you?" The officer waved Luke to step away from Charlotte.

"Sure thing." He looked at Charlotte. "I'll be right back."

"Mr. Anderson, I just wanted to say that Ms. Cavanaugh is probably in shock, so she shouldn't be left alone for a while."

"Thanks for the advice. I appreciate it." Luke made his way back to Charlotte and supported her as she stepped down from the ambulance. As they walked to his truck, he kept one arm around her and the other holding her hand.

"I feel silly with you hovering over me. It's not like I was hurt or anything."

"Of course you weren't. I just needed some reassurance that you're fine. That's all." He held open the passenger door and helped her up into the seat. Driving away, Luke looked back at the house thanking the saints in heaven because it could have been so much worse.

"I'm going to take you to my place, so I can get you something to eat. And so you can relax. If you tell me who you want me to call, I can notify people for you."

Luke continued talking about how happy he was that she wasn't hurt, and how it didn't look that terrible from the outside. Luke parked the truck. Charlotte hadn't said much during the ten minute ride to his house.

Supporting Charlotte close to his side, he unlocked the front door. One hand on her elbow, Luke escorted her to the couch. "I'll put on some soup and get you a cup of tea." She just nodded.

"I should call my parents."

"You can use that phone on the end table. I'll be right back."

At the arch separating the kitchen from the living room Luke waited, giving Charlotte the space she needed. With two shaking hands she cradled the portable phone and dialed. She hesitated while the phone rang. He could hear a voice on the phone, then a beep, then an answering machine. "Hi Mom, Dad. I'll try again later." She placed the phone back on the table and sat back, staring up to the ceiling, visibly stunned.

When he brought her the hot tea, she looked up and he realized her lip was quivering and her eyes were red. He couldn't believe how stupid he'd been to leave her alone. He put the teacup down and sat.

She threw herself onto his lap and wrapped her arms around him in a death grip. Whole body sobs tore from her, and Luke's heart broke. He just held on tightly and let her release all the tension she had tried so valiantly to hide from him.

"I was so s-scared. At f-first I was mad someone trashed the house. Then I heard the w-window break and I saw the fire burst out. I don't even know how I knew the fire extinguisher was there on the counter. I just moved and sprayed and it was over. It happened so fast, and I don't u-understand why I can't stop shaking."

Luke reached for an afghan blanket his mom had made for him. He wrapped Charlotte in it to see if it would help to calm her nerves.

Buzzing from timer on the stove notified him the soup was ready. "Honey, I'm just going to the kitchen to get your soup. I'll be right back."

She nodded and he reluctantly left her, returning moments later with some hot tomato soup. "I put it in a mug so you can sip on it."

"Thank you." She placed one palm on his cheek. Wet eyelashes and still flush from the adrenalin rush, she couldn't have looked more enchanting. "You've been so sweet to me."

"You can't imagine how crazed I felt when I heard what had happened. We'd just been standing in the same room, and then I heard you were in a fire. I couldn't get to you fast enough. Do you want to talk about what happened?"

She lifted one shoulder in a half shrug. He was surprised when she started to speak. "I had inspected the family room, where all the drywall damage was done by the vandals. I was in the kitchen. I heard a noise and looked out the window. I saw a silver Lexus drive off. Isn't it weird I remember that? It took me a few seconds before I realized the fire was spreading across the floor. The cabinets were burning. The black smoke made it so hard to breathe. Then, that's when I noticed the fire extinguisher. In my mind I put the fire out in seconds, but it probably took minutes. Once the flames were gone I just stood there, not moving, for what seemed like an hour. I got myself together and that was when I called 911. It was a blur, yet so focused and clear, all at the same time. Even now I find it hard to believe I even went through that today."

"I hate that you went through it. I don't think my heart started beating again until I saw you sitting there in the ambulance. I just … I'm just so happy you're all right." One arm around her, he hugged her close.

"Me too." Charlotte put her head on his shoulder.

"Drink up. There's no rush. We can just sit here and relax. How about a movie?"

She nodded. "Sure. Whatever you want. Well, anything that doesn't involve a burning building would be great."

They laughed. Charlotte drank from her mug of soup while Luke looked through the movie options. He started a movie. It was the first he found that he thought would be safe to watch.

"I was thinking about *Four Weddings and a Funeral*, but I went for the traditional 80s hit *Sixteen Candles* as a safer option."

She leaned over and gave him a quick kiss on the lips. "Thank you. It's perfect."

Charlotte snuggled into his side as he wrapped his arm around her holding her close. They watched the movie while she finished her soup.

Mid-movie Luke quietly talked. "When my mother was sick I would make her soup and watch movies with her. She said it was nice to have someone take care of her for a change. I never minded. She also said she was sorry she wouldn't get to see me as a father. She would have been a wonderful grandmother. Those quiet times can't be replaced. They're good memories, happy ones." Charlotte hadn't responded. Looking down, her eyelashes fanning out along the tops of her cheeks reminded Luke of a more peaceful time. Another time not long ago he was able to hold her and watch her sleep... Her small hand slid over his chest, stopping on his heart. Her even breathing reassured him that the stress of the day was fading away.

***

Sunlight pierced her eyelids and a pang of panic washed over her when she didn't recognize her surroundings. Then she felt the heat from Luke's body and the weight of his arm holding her in place. With a quick check, she realized she still had on her clothes. Her shoes had been removed, but a vague memory came back of leaving them by the back door, watching the movie and Luke telling her about his mother as she fell asleep.

Slowly, so she didn't disturb him, she eased herself out from the warmth of his embrace. Charlotte stood on the side of the bed regretting leaving her place in his arms, but she knew it was for the best.

He'd been so sweet to her the night before, and she could've easily stayed with him. He took over. Helping her recover from the shock of the fire. He had taken over at her future home, cleaning out the library, too. She hadn't asked for his help. Can she allow herself to be taken care of like that? Charlotte liked being in charge of her own life. It was nice, very nice to have a friend to lean on, but was Luke too much? She needed time to figure things out.

Before she second guessed her decision, she left his house.

Chapter Twenty

CHARLOTTE FOCUSED ON the client folder open on her desk, but the slight air movement from the door opening had her look up. Jessica stood in the doorway, wide eyed, with a man holding a gun to the side of her head. He had at least a day's worth of facial hair. His eyes scanned quickly one side of the room, then the other. In all the years she had known him, lived with him, Grant had never looked like this . . . crazy.

"Get in there." He hit Jessica on the back of the head with the gun and pushed her so she fell to her knees, whimpering. Charlotte moved to stand to go to her.

"Don't move. I just need you to listen to me." His voice cracked. Fear. Charlotte couldn't be sure. The gun waved back and forth, and the only thing Charlotte focused on was his finger placed on the trigger.

Shaking, Charlotte's thoughts scattered. Trying to focus, she said the only thing she could. Her mouth dried up, and the idea that she was dreaming kept her from completely losing control. "What are you doing? Why don't we sit down?"

"No!"

A control she wasn't confident she could express rose up. She lifted both hands, palms out in surrender. "Can I please make sure Jessica's okay?"

"No! This is all your fault. If you would have just stayed with me. Had fun with me. Come home with me! None of this would be happening!" He paced a few steps. The more he spoke the louder he yelled. The louder he yelled, the more wildly he moved the gun around with the swinging of his hands.

Sweat dripped down his forehead. Light bounced off the greasy sheen of his hair. Never before had Charlotte observed Grant in such an unkempt state. Large wet sweat marks stained the dress shirt. The same shirt he wore the night of the benefit. It hung untucked from his wrinkled trousers. Charlotte retreated a step and crossed her arms over her middle. Jessica whimpered uncontrollably, rocking back and forth. If only she could check on her to make sure she wasn't seriously hurt.

"Well, I have a problem with your new boyfriend. He can't just take you from me. We had our problems, but you were coming back to me. You went to the benefit with ME! You were going home with ME!" He has to pay for what he has done."

"You want him to pay?"

He rushed toward her and shoved her against the wall. The hard surface forced the air from her lungs while her head slammed into it. He walked back a few steps.

"Why did you make me do that? You've always been very quick. Yes, he has to pay. No one can treat me like that and not pay."

Piercing pain shot through the back of her head. "Grant, this is crazy." The sound of her own voice caused more pain. Charlotte held her head with both hands. "I told you I was going to the benefit, but it wasn't a date. I told you we weren't getting back together."

"You went with ME! It was a date!"

"Okay, okay." Her shaking legs could no longer hold her up. Charlotte sat back down in her desk chair. "I made a mistake. Let's let Jessica go back to her desk, and we can talk about this."

"Sure whatever." He waved the gun toward the door, pointing the way for Jessica to leave.

Wide eyed panic raced across Jessica's face. Charlotte sat and helplessly watched as her friend gained her footing and backed out of the room. Charlotte knew in her gut if Grant moved to hurt Jessica she would jump him. He didn't move and Jessica was safe.

Grant walked to the door and turned the lock. The smirk on his lips had once been a sign of mischief. At this moment, she only felt sick. "Oh, my dear. This whole thing can be done and over with. All you have to do is say you will come back to me." The gun no longer waved haphazardly around the room. No, this calm person standing before her, a gun at his side, was much more chilling. "Just agree that you made a mistake in leaving me, and this whole mess can be resolved."

"I made a mistake?"

He walked closer. Leaning over her, Charlotte could smell the foul stench of body odor mixed with alcohol from his breath. "Have you been drinking?"

"You think I'd show up at your office without a little liquid courage?"

Her eyes darted around the room. She had to do something to get herself out of the office. "You look tired. Why don't you have a seat? I can get you a water?" She put her hands on the arms of her chair as if to stand.

"Stay! Just stay." He sat in a chair across from her. "I'm tired, Charlotte." Grant's voice wavered. Peering closely, really studying him, Charlotte saw the shadows and dark circles around his eyes. Sadness? Maybe. "You left and I thought everything would be fine. Then you moved your things out. Then you didn't come back. Seeing you talking with him killed something in me."

"You know this is wrong, right?"

"I should just go, right?" He looked over his shoulder.

"Let me call your doctor. He can give you something to help you sleep. Maybe some rest will give you a better perspective."

"No!" Abruptly he stood and rushed to the door. "You can't stay with him Charlotte. I won't let you." He put the gun in the waist of his pants and flipped his shirt over it to hide it. "Things will be different this time for us. You'll see." And he left.

Stunned by his departure, Charlotte jumped when Jessica rushed back into her office and fell into her arms sobbing.

"I called the police. I didn't know what to do! I went into the closet and waited till I heard him leave."

Charlotte looked directly into her friends eyes. "Are you sure he left?" With an overwhelming need for safety, Charlotte lowered Jessica to the floor and ran to lock them into her office.

Jessica rolled to her side in a fetal position and wept. The coolness on her back from the wooden door added a welcome relief as she slid to the floor. Tears flowed freely down Charlotte's face. "I can't believe that just happened." Cold seeped into her very soul and her whole body trembled.

Jessica sat up, holding her knees to her chest. "Do you think Grant will come back?"

"I … I have no idea." Charlotte put her shaking finger to her lips. "Shhh, I hear someone out in the lobby."

Loud knocking shook the door at Charlotte's back. Holding her head, Charlotte wished the person screaming would stop. Opening her eyes, it dawned on her that she was the one making the noise. She stopped. Jessica just covered her own mouth with both of her hands.

The door handle moved up and down. "Charlotte, Charlotte open the door, it's Luke."

Relief poured from her at the realization it was Luke's voice she was hearing. She rolled to her knees and reached to open the door. She was still behind the door preventing Luke from entering fully.

"Charlotte, are you behind the door?"

"Yes, let me …" Charlotte moved further back and felt the couch behind her. Both hands gripped the seat cushion and she pulled herself up to sit on it.

Luke entered the room and stared at Jessica on the floor. Charlotte felt the lump in her throat as she took in her friend's appearance for the first time. Red rimmed eyes, swollen from crying, Jessica appeared otherwise unharmed.

The moment he looked directly at her, his eyes widened in surprise. Luke's mouth dropped open, but he didn't speak right away. "What the hell happened?" He ran over and kneeled at her feet.

"Grant. He was here. With a gun. Didn't you see him?" Charlotte pointed to the door.

"No. Stay put." He pulled his cellphone from his back pocket dialing numbers. "I need to report an assault." He listened. "Yes, send an ambulance, too. The Century Two building, first floor, suite one-ten." His eyes moved from looking at Charlotte to looking at Jessica. Luke continued to give his assessment of the scene. "I think only minor injuries."

His voice faded as her own thoughts wandered. How could this be happening? Charlotte had been in a relationship with Grant for the last few years. Up until his indiscretion he had not only been her best friend, but also a business confidant.

"Charlotte, I already called 911." Charlotte stopped her hands from unlocking her cellphone. She needed to act, react. What was the right thing to be doing?

The whole situation had played out like a movie. The only problem Charlotte could see was that she was the star. The role of a lifetime she wished she hadn't been cast in.

The screech of a siren could already be heard in the distance. Luke continued to talk on the phone. He spoke but Charlotte didn't really hear.

"Jess, are you hurt?" Charlotte realized she hadn't yet asked her friend how she was doing. The rough texture of the carpeting abraded her knees as she knelt next to Jessica. They hugged each other.

"I think I'm okay. My head hurts and my eyes hurt." Jessica put both hands on her face. "I can feel they're puffy, but I think I'm okay."

Lifting her hand and stroking Jessica's head, Charlotte felt something sticky. Red streaks of blood on her palm froze her in place for a moment before she could find her voice. "Oh no, Jess. Your head is bleeding. Let me look."

"That would explain the headache."

Several police officers swept into the room along with a few paramedics. Luke stepped back so the women could be helped.

An officer stepped over to Charlotte and Jessica. "Once we know you're well enough, I'd like to ask you some questions."

Charlotte and Jessica agreed. Charlotte stood to get the officer's attention. "The gentleman that called arrived after the person who threatened us had left. I just wanted to make sure you didn't think he did this."

"Thank you for that information. I'll find you after you're all fixed up."

The paramedic used a flashlight to shine in her eyes, checked her blood pressure, which was elevated but not dangerously high and evaluated the back of her head when she told them she had been pushed into the wall.

Another paramedic stepped over, the one who had been helping Jessica. "Ms. Cavanaugh, we will be transporting your friend to the hospital for further evaluation on her head wound."

"Thank you. I was worried about that. I only realized she was bleeding right before you arrived. If you don't think I need to go, then I'd like to stay here with the police."

"That's fine, but we recommend you see your primary care physician if you start to feel dizzy or sick to your stomach."

Nervous laughter escaped. "Thank you for the advice and for coming so quickly."

Jessica was placed on a stretcher that Charlotte hadn't even realized was in her office. She walked to the door and watched as Jessica was wheeled out of the office. "Wait a second." She walked quickly to her friend and held her hand. Looking down, Charlotte spoke quietly. "Jessica, call me. I'll come and get you to bring you home." They hugged once more. This time, as she stepped back, she watched the gurney roll out of the office.

Luke looked up as Charlotte approached him. "You should have gone to the hospital."

"I should have installed security cameras, so I'd have video evidence of this. Instead, one of my best friends is on the way to the hospital, and I can hardly believe Grant has flipped out to the point that he hit her over the head with a gun and is now running around town."

"What?" Both the officer and Luke asked loudly.

"Ms. Cavanaugh, maybe you should have a seat and tell me exactly what happened. You know who did this?" Luke walked her over to a loveseat and they sat down with his arm around her. The officer sat on a chair, too.

Tensing, she retold the story of Grant's forced entry into the office. Charlotte worked to keep her emotions in check.

They needed to know what happened. "He crowded me at my desk when he told me breaking up was a mistake. He looked crazy. His eyes, they were wild."

"What did you say this guy's name is?" The officer hesitated in his notetaking.

"The guy is Grant Becker. He lives here in town. This is so fucked up. He cheated on me." She ran her hand through her hair in frustration. "This is why I don't need a man in my life."

Luke swore under his breath and stood. Pacing, he ran his hand through his hair. "I think that what happened with Becker is a mess. But you need time to calm down."

Charlotte couldn't believe she was hearing this. He was partly to blame. He had put on that show in the diner in front of Grant. He had made a scene at the benefit when he knew she was there with Grant.

The officer stood. "Mr. Anderson, I think maybe Miss Cavanaugh needs some space."

"Is that what you want?" Luke stood and walked a few steps away before turning to the officer, but looked directly at Charlotte. "I'm glad you will be okay, Charlotte. You know how to contact me if you need anything."

The officer stepped between Charlotte and Luke. "Sir, I think I need you to come down to the station to make an official statement. We may need clearer details of what happened. From your point of view."

"Anything." Peering around the officer their eyes met. "Charlotte?" She looked away. "Call me."

Sadness settled in her bones. Grant lied to Charlotte and she caught him cheating. Doubt about her own decisions when it came to men crept in. Luke had been so kind and likeable, and sweet and handsome and Charlotte found that she could have easily fallen for him. She needed to talk with him, but having him in her life in a romantic capacity just couldn't happen. She was putting herself in a timeout from dating. Something she should have done before. "I'm going to get Jessica and bring her home and then just head right to my place."

"You should call someone, too. Maybe instead of trying to do everything alone, you could call your parents. That's what they are there for."

Feeling stronger and determined to put him and this mess behind her, she stood and finally looked at Luke. "I can manage. Go, do what you have to do. I'll sort out my own things."

Luke stepped toward the door and looked back one last time and left. The ringing of her cell phone made her jump, and she realized her nerves were more shot than she thought.

One of the two officers still in her office directed her to answer her phone while it was on speaker phone.

She acknowledged that she understood. Depressing the button and quickly putting the call on speaker, Charlotte sat in her desk chair. "Hello."

"Hi Charlotte. It's Aimee. So, my brother just called me and said I needed to call you. He said Luke Anderson told him to relay the message. Can you tell me why I'm calling you?"

Realization snapped in place and Charlotte took her friend off speaker. "Hi Aim, it's a long story. Can you come by my office? I'm pretty sure I shouldn't be driving, and I need to head over to the hospital to pick up Jessica."

"What?" Aimee yelled into the phone.

"I'll explain when you get here. There are a few things I need to clear up before I can leave."

Chapter Twenty-One

THE BRICK FRONT police station had been standing since the mid-fifties according to the corner stone. The flag snapped from the breeze and the sun shone all the way up the sidewalk to the front door. Luke followed the path into the building.

He was greeted by the officer that had been at Charlotte's office. "Mr. Anderson, thank you for following me down here. I don't think I introduced myself properly before. I'm Officer Lewis, and over there is Detective Klein." Officer Lewis pointed to a nearby colleague. "He will be sitting in while you tell us what has been happening. The Captain said we can use the conference room."

Luke stepped into the room and immediately sensed it wasn't an interrogation room, but indeed a conference room. His casual pace, silenced by the carpeting and the leather cushioned chairs, eased his tense body as he sat patiently waiting for the other men to gather the supplies they needed.

"Mr. Anderson, I'm Detective Klein." He sat down to Luke's right. "Is it okay for me to record this conversation for us to reference later?"

"Sure."

"Good, I like to have the recording." Detective Klein placed the small device on the table between them. It appeared he was going to be in charge of the meeting. "I understand you are a witness to the incident at Ms. Cavanaugh's office?"

"Yes." Luke looked between the two men. Officer Lewis was now seated to Luke's left.

"Can you elaborate for Officer Lewis and me, so that we can get a better picture of how you fit into all of this?"

"Of course." Luke cleared his throat. "I arrived at Ms. Cavanaugh's office. Jessica wasn't at her desk in the reception area. I walked back and Ms. Cavanaugh's door was shut. I knocked and heard muffled voices. When I tried to enter, something blocked the way. Listen, you guys came in only a few minutes after me. This thing with Grant Becker has been escalating for a while. Ms. Cavanaugh had a personal and professional relationship with the guy. He's bent out of shape because she ended the personal part. I was with her when he threatened her in the diner across town a couple mornings ago."

"You have no doubt that Mr. Becker did this?"

"None." Luke clasped his hands. "The last time I saw the guy with her, he was not happy. Let's just say he seemed like he had hopes they would get back together."

Both detectives wrote notes down. Luke's phone vibrated in his pocket. He pulled it out looking at the screen.

The three men listened to the messages. They all said the same thing until the last one.

Eighth missed call.

"I have had enough of this game. I have been watching you. I see you're playing games with her. Maybe I should go pay her a visit. Maybe she doesn't know how you're using her. I will have her back."

Fear raced down Luke's spine at how ugly things could have turned out in Charlotte's office. Luke received several odd messages, but hadn't thought anything about them. Now, now he knew who left them. The seriousness of the calls started to sink in. The maniac that had been leaving these messages had been following him long enough to know about his relationship, friendship, meetings with Charlotte. Now he knew Grant Becker was that maniac.

"Mr. Anderson, you don't look good. Can we get you some water?"

Realizing the officer was talking to him, Luke declined the offer. "No, I'll be okay. That last message made me realize just how sick this guy is. Charlotte and Jessica could have been hurt a lot worse."

"Can you think of any other reason why Grant Becker would have reacted like this?"

With a heavy sigh, Luke used his cell phone to look up a phone number. "The guy was bothering Charlotte. I knew they had just broken up. Charlotte and I work together on some houses and she asked me for advice for a house she was thinking of buying. The place we met up at, the diner, Becker was there, and I acted like Charlotte and I were a couple. Just to piss him off. This is all my fault. If I had kept my nose out of her private life he would have faded away. Instead I egged him on."

Detective Klein took the cell phone and wrote down the number Grant used to call Luke. It wasn't Grant's business number. "We'll find Mr. Becker and bring him in. In the meantime if he contacts you again let us know."

"Thanks. Do you need me to stay anymore? I'd like to check on Charlotte."

"No, go ahead. We'll contact you if we have any further questions. "Don't worry. We've started a list of charges for this guy."

"Thanks." Luke shook hands with the two men and left the police station.

The sun was below the tree line casting shadows across the parking lot. The evening air was beginning to chill, and an urgent need to make sure Charlotte was safe and secure for the evening became Luke's number one priority. He found her cell phone number and called as he walked toward his truck. He slid his hand into his pants pocket and gripped the rough edges of the keys.

As soon as the phone was answered Luke started talking, needing to reassure himself she was safe. "Charlotte, where are you? I'm coming over."

"Luke, I'm back at the hotel. Aimee came and got me and we picked up Jessica. I'm extremely tired. I think all the excitement wiped me out. I'll be fine. I just want to relax."

"I need to make sure you're all right." Luke was desperate to be sure she was all right.

"I'm fine. I still have to call my parents, and then I'm just going to bed."

"I think we need to talk …" She cut him off before he could continue the conversation.

"I need time to process what has been happening. I'll call you when I'm up for a conversation. Goodnight, Luke." And she hung up.

"Goodnight Charlotte." Luke spoke to the disconnected phone. Everything had changed between them in an instant and Luke felt desperate to mend any conflicts Charlotte had with him. He wasn't a cheater like Grant, and he hadn't been looking for a relationship with her, but it had found him. Was Charlotte just one more person that would leave him, proving it wasn't worth the heartache?

***

The beer sat full, beads of sweat dripping down the glass, puddling on the bar top. Luke continued to stare into the amber liquid knowing his friend was directly in front of him with his arms folded, waiting for him to flinch in the non-verbal standoff they had started.

"Are you going to sulk all night over one beer, or are you going to fix whatever your problem is?"

"Shut it." Luke was in a foul mood; he didn't feel like dealing with anyone. The idea that Charlotte thought he could be shoved aside, she didn't need him, or he hadn't started to need her was absurd. He didn't run from trouble. He was the one that waited, held his mother's hand while she lay dying. He was the person that stepped up when his friends needed anything. Now look at where he was for his kindness!

"This is stupid." Luke threw a twenty on the bar and pushed off his seat. "Nice guys finish last, my ass. I'm gonna change that."

Jim just kept standing there with his arms folded. "Ok tiger, go get 'em. Whatever it is you're getting."

Luke gave a wave over his shoulder as he pushed out the bar door. The cool night air hit his face as his boots crunched on pebbles along the concrete sidewalk. Halfway to his truck a searing pain raced across his shoulders, and he fell to his knees. Clanking of a metal bat landing on the ground was followed by more pain erupting as a fist connected with his jaw when he looked back. Luke rolled to his back and kicked his booted foot toward the shadowed figure. He missed and his assailant grabbed his shirt and connected with his face once again.

Luke latched onto the hoodie and hit the guy in the head. "What the hell are you doing?"

The guy spat in his face. "You can't have her. She made a mistake and I'm here to correct that." He punched Luke again.

"What the hell are you talking about?!" Anger coursed through Luke as he gained his footing. In his upright position he was much larger than the guy. Like a lightbulb going off, Luke knew in that instant who attacked him. "Becker? You stupid ass. You cheated on Charlotte. She doesn't want to be with you anymore, you idiot. Let it go. This isn't high school."

Grant stopped moving, then raised his hands higher. "You're a liar. She does want to be with me. She went to the benefit with me. When I started that fire it scared her, and now she wants to come back to me."

"And she went home with me. Get over it. Wait? You did what?"

The back door of the bar burst open and Jim ran with a bat in hand. The noise had Grant turning around. When he saw the hulking figure barreling toward him, Grant took off running into the darkness.

Holding himself up with his hands on his knees, Luke was panting. "How the hell did you know?"

"I have security cameras in the parking lot. I just happened to look up and saw you on the ground."

"Yeah, he got the drop on me. At least I know who it was." Luke shook his head and stood straight. "The cops are gonna love me. Twice in one day. Maybe they will deputize me."

They both laughed. "You want me to drive you?"

"Thanks Jim, but I'm good. I'll be sore in the morning, but I'm good for now."

"Ok man, but if you need anything let me know."

Chapter Twenty-Two

FOR THE FIRST time in a very long time, Charlotte screened her calls. When her mother's name flashed, she needed to talk. "Hi, Mom."

"How are you? Your baby misses you."

"I'm fine, Mom. I tried to call. You must have been out. Has Dad been spoiling Sam?"

"He won't ever be the same again after this visit."

"I'm sure he is getting the royal treatment, and I'll have to break him of all the bad manners his grandparents are teaching him." That brought about a laugh from both of them.

"You know I want you to move home."

"Thanks Mom, I'm fine. Things are looking good for getting a new home. I only have a few other things that need to get cleared up, but I'm close to getting a house."

"Fine, if that's all I get then I'll keep your baby spoiled till you can retrieve him. I'm going to make a roast with lots of gravy just for your pooch."

"Oh gosh, Mom. He will never want to come and live with me again. Maybe I'll have a chat with him about all the birds he'll be able to chase living there. Isn't that how you get kids to do stuff? Bribe them?

"I hope I taught you more than bribing to get your way. You probably need to get back to work. We'll talk again soon."

"You're right. I should probably get some work done. Love you." Her intercom immediately buzzed.

"Charlotte, Mrs. Camden is here to see you with a police officer."

"Thank you, Jessica. Please show them to my office."

The door opened and Mrs. Camden entered, followed by an officer in uniform. Jessica closed the door behind them.

"Mrs. Camden, Officer ...?"

"Hadley."

"Have a seat." Charlotte waved to the chairs in front of her desk. "Can I get you anything to drink—water, coffee?"

"No, thank you. I don't mean to intrude." Mrs. Camden sat down.

Charlotte sat behind her desk.

"Ms. Cavanaugh, Mrs. Camden asked me to come with her today. She asked me to allow her to explain the circumstances behind the vandalism at her home."

"Oh, I see." Charlotte looked from Mrs. Camden to Officer Hadley. Confused was more like it though.

"No. I don't think you could possibly see." Mrs. Camden visibly swallowed and closed her eyes. When she opened them sadness radiated. "You see, Ms. Cavanaugh, I—that is, my husband and I—we owe you a huge apology."

"An apology?"

"Yes. The thing is, Ms. Cavanaugh," Mrs. Camden cleared her throat, her eyes rimmed red. "Everything that happened the other day was because of us. My marriage was based on this illusion of greatness. Don't get me wrong. I love my husband beyond belief, and somehow I've even forgiven him, but it was because he thought I needed a showplace of a house to be happy that we were building that monstrosity. My husband hasn't worked in over six months." She choked back a sob. "I had no idea, and even worse, because he hadn't told me, I was unsuspectingly spending our retirement money to build and decorate this new house. A new house just to keep a status symbol." She stopped and caught herself before a sob escaped. "You see, it was my husband who ransacked the house. To scare me, and you, too. If I had just said I would wait then you wouldn't have been involved. My husband couldn't see past his thoughts of failing our family to see how we love him no matter what. We have no idea how the fire started, but it was my husband who damaged the house in the first place.

Charlotte had been staring at Mrs. Camden. She squeezed her hands together so hard her fingertips turned white. "I know Mr. Camden was concerned about the expense. I'm so sorry about everything." Charlotte didn't know what else to say; she was having a hard time processing that a person would do such a thing.

Mrs. Camden wiped her eyes with a tissue Charlotte handed her. "It's me who's sorry. If my husband had said to just stop everything then you wouldn't have been at the house checking on it when the fire started. I'd understand if you wanted to press charges. My husband never thought of harming you. He wasn't thinking straight. He … he's a mess with guilt. He thought the home invasion would scare you off. He needed time to figure out how to pay for the things we agreed to do. He thought if you quit working for us, I'd be stumped about what to do next, and he'd have more time to find a new job." Mrs. Camden started to cry. "If he would've just told me about losing his job none of this would have happened."

Charlotte found herself crying. "As crazy as this story is, I think I understand Mr. Camden's logic. I can't imagine how he felt at the thought of disappointing you. The desperation he felt. I don't condone his actions, but I think I understand them." Charlotte stood.

Officer Hadley cleared his throat. "There is more. We have information that should lead to an arrest of the arsonist at the Camden's home. I can't give you any more information at this time, but I just wanted you to know."

"Thank you. That's good to know." She stood.

Officer Hadley and Mrs. Camden stood, as well. "Mr. Camden is being questioned down at the station right now. We have our own charges against him. Ms. Cavanaugh, if you have any questions or plan on pressing charges, please give me a call. I assume you'll need some time to think things over."

"Yes, thank you." Charlotte took the business card and walked them to her office door. "Mrs. Camden, I want to say that I appreciate you coming to tell me this yourself. I'm glad to see the relationship I developed with you is just as important to you as it is to me."

Mrs. Camden hugged Charlotte quickly and left the office with tears in her eyes, followed by Officer Hadley.

Jessica entered. "Soooo, are you going to share what happened?"

"This story requires a strong drink. I'll text Aimee and have her join us too, so I don't have to repeat this a million times. Let's close up shop and head to a bar."

***

Luke sat in the shadows of the far back side of Jim's bar as Charlotte and her assistant Jessica found a booth. Jim's sister Aimee walked in just a minute later. "Should I send over one of those funny shots again?" Jim asked with a goofy grin on his face.

"Nah, I'm giving Charlotte some space. She's been through a lot. I'm stepping back so she can get her bearings."

"That's a pretty noble gesture. You must have a thing for her."

Luke looked at the bar top. "I do. I just wish I could say it was reciprocated."

"Ok, I guess I'll let you hide over here."

Luke watched as Jim approached their table, made some small talk and took their order. The waitress placed Luke's dinner plate in front of him and he shoved some French fries into his mouth to keep from asking Jim what the girls talked about.

"So, don't you want to know what Charlotte said to me?"

"No, I'm not in high school."

"I guess not. I guess you won't mind that I've got a date with her tomorrow night either?"

"Now you're just being a jerk."

"Maybe I am, but you didn't say I couldn't ask her." Jim stepped back at the look on Luke's face. "Okay, okay. I didn't ask her out. What gives?"

"Man ..." Luke pushed his uneaten burger away. "It's been a week since I saw her. She was in this house fire, and I brought her back to my place so she wouldn't be alone." At the odd look on Jim's face, Luke quickly clarified. "Nothing happened. I wouldn't take advantage of someone after something like that. Give me a little credit. I made her some soup and put on a sappy eighties movie. She fell asleep, and when I woke up she was gone. I went to check on her at work, and she had just been threatened. Now, I haven't heard one word from her. The dude that attacked me in your parking lot is the same guy that went after her. He's her ex, the one that cheated on her and now is determined to get her back."

"Reality check, a lot of guys would do that. They catch the guy yet?"

Luke had a hard time believing Grant elude the police for long. "No, but they'll get him."

"She must have been freaked out about that fire. Maybe giving her some time is a good idea. Let her make the choice to contact you. You know that old saying ... how does it go? 'Absence makes the heart grow fonder'."

"Yeah, I've been trying that. I've gotta tell ya, man. I'm about done with waiting, though. We'll both be at this meeting tomorrow. At least, I think she's going to be there. Anyhow,

I'm hoping I can talk to her then, or afterward." Luke looked over at the girls. Charlotte was leaning over the table, talking to Jessica. "I should go. I don't want Charlotte to think I was spying or anything like that."

"Sure. But I don't think she'd think that about you, even if she did see you. Good luck."

"Thanks Jim." Luke stood and pulled out his wallet and threw some money down for his uneaten food. They fist-bumped and Luke headed out the back of the bar. He was trying his best to respect Charlotte's space, but he needed to talk with her. Tomorrow, after the closing on the sale of the house, she was going to have to hear him out.

***

In the dark back corner of the bar, she saw Jim fist-bump someone who was leaving. Aimee cleared her throat to catch her attention. "Have you talked with Luke since you left his place?"

Suddenly her fingers were very important, and Charlotte started pressing back her cuticles. "No. I stayed with him after the fire, and then after Grant came to the office he came to talk. To say the least, I was freaked out. I might have said something to the effect that men aren't worth it. It's weird how I miss him so much. I shouldn't, right? This wasn't supposed to be a thing. Then he goes and makes things messy by being so perfect and now I miss him."

Jessica reached for her hand. "Honey, you can never tell when Cupid is going to get you with that arrow. You two should talk things out."

"I know. We will, but right now I just need to think."

"You know that Jessica and I are here for you for anything. You don't even have to ask. But I should get going. I've got a super long day tomorrow." Aimee said.

"It's been a crazy day," Charlotte agreed. "I need to get some sleep, too."

The three women left their booth and headed toward their cars. Aimee and Jessica left the parking lot before Charlotte pulled out of her space. A car pulled into the lot and stopped behind Charlotte's car. Grant.

Gritting her teeth, Charlotte grabbed her cell phone and got out of her car before she knew what she was doing. A moment of sanity did step in, and she hit the dial button on her phone, and then put the phone on speaker. Heart pounding and hands shaking she decided this confrontation had to happen right now. "Grant, this has got to stop. You can't come into my office and abuse me or Jessica, and then expect me to stop what I'm doing to chat with you. You need to go talk to the police."

The car door opened and Grant stood before her in a concert t-shirt and jeans. Beads of sweat dotted his forehead. Did she ever really know this person? How could this be the same man?

Grant approached her. "I'm sorry about before. I wasn't thinking. I just … I just want you back home. I just need to talk to you. I made a mess of things, and I want to make it right."

Her whole body vibrated as Charlotte contemplated how she should proceed. "I've called someone to let him know

you are here. You need to take responsibility for what you
have done."

He clenched his hands and took a single step toward her
and stopped. "I messed up. I just want things back the way
they were."

"You don't get to have everything you want. It's not just
all about you. I get to have a choice here, and my choice is
not to be with you."

Tires crunching caught the attention of Charlotte and
Grant. Luke's truck sped into the parking lot followed closely
by a police car.

"You called him?"

"Yes, and he must have called the police. The way you
are acting needs to stop right here."

"I'm sorry, Charlotte." He didn't resist as the police officer cuffed him.

She watched as he was assisted into the back of the police car. Charlotte knew that Luke stood beside her. His
warmth and support eased the tension, and bone tired exhaustion settled in.

"Are you okay?"

"I am. I'm just very tired." Still standing watching the
scene unfold around them, Charlotte didn't face Luke. "I just
need to go to sleep."

"I'll get that car moved and see what you need to do."

"Thanks."

Only a few minutes had gone by, but time moved in a
weird blur. Father Time moved the clock forward then back,
fast then slow. Sleep couldn't come fast enough.

"I convinced the police to take your statement tomorrow. Here sit in your car." Charlotte felt the hand at her back, then the soft comfort of her leather seats. "Are you sure you're okay to drive back?"

"I'll be okay. It's a short drive."

"I'm going to follow you. Just to make sure you make it there. We can talk tomorrow, too."

"I think we should." Luke turned to leave, but Charlotte needed to say one more thing. "Luke …" He turned back. "Thank you for everything."

"My pleasure. Don't forget to buckle up." Charlotte closed her car door and smiled. Grant was no longer going to bother her, and if nothing else, Luke just might remain a friend at the very least.

Chapter Twenty-Three

HER MOTHER'S WORDS echoed as she drove toward the next step in her future. Charlotte enjoyed lunch with her parents earlier in the day. Sam was now the most spoiled dog, or fur grandbaby, as her mother called him, on his stay-cation at her parent's house. Her father was out of the loop, so the conversation around the table turned into a confession about how Charlotte hadn't wanted to disappoint them with the news she had broken off her relationship with Grant. Her father held her hand to reassure her. "You know we love you and only want to see you happy."

"I know, Dad. I think what I've come to realize is that you weren't putting the pressure on me to get married and have children. That was a dream I wanted for myself."

Reflecting on that realization as she walked into the closing of her new home, Charlotte paused, surprised to find Luke sitting at the table. Several times she had picked up the phone to talk, to work out her feelings toward him, but she just hadn't been able to do it.

The green and yellow of healing bruises weren't enough to disguise his handsome face. The thought of him in a fight stunned her. Then again, she hadn't exactly been very observant of the actions of anyone around her.

Charlotte's realtor pulled out a chair for her. The in control Charlotte Cavanaugh, suddenly, unsure of herself, said a general hello to the occupants of the table.

The title agent began the proceedings by introducing everyone. "Ms. Cavanaugh, this is the person you'll be buying your new home from, Luke Anderson."

"Mr. Anderson, thank you for allowing me to be the keeper of this home. I'll cherish every nook and cranny."

"That, Ms. Cavanaugh, is exactly why I think you're the perfect person for me to sell to."

The truth of his words hit the mark. From the moment Charlotte met Luke he had supported her and showed her his true self. He never spoke to impress, put on airs. Luke Anderson was a genuine person. Which made it even more of a surprise he hadn't shared the truth about owning the house. There was a story and Charlotte was curious to find out what it was.

Charlotte knew Luke watched her as she signed her name more times than she cared to ever do again. Pen in hand, his hand moved swiftly as he signed the few documents he needed to for the property transfer, and then everything was complete. She could finally get out of the hotel and retrieve her things from storage. She finally had a place to call home.

Luke got to the conference room door first and held it for Charlotte and her realtor. The two women left the title agency together.

Charlotte stood on the sidewalk, looking into her handbag. "Charlotte."

"Hi, I can't seem to find my keys in this bottomless pit of a bag." Her face pressed into the outer edges as one hand moved items around inside the oversized purse.

"I was wondering if you'd like to have a cup of coffee with me." His voice resonated with a calm that reassured her.

She looked up, keys dangling from one finger. "Yes, that'd be nice. I have a few things I need to tell you."

"All right. I'll meet you at the diner?"

"I'll be right behind you."

***

Charlotte arrived first and waited for Luke outside the diner, enjoying the warmth of the sun. He held open the diner's door and they were greeted by the silver-haired owner.

"Just the two of you?"

"Just us." Just the two of them. More than ever that idea felt right. Like the blanket you reach for on a cold winter night. That warmth, wrapped around you, making everything else in the world second best.

It was between breakfast and lunch, so only a few seats were taken. Luke didn't open the menu. "Go ahead and order whatever you'd like. This is a celebration of your independence and homeownership."

"I thought I was pretty independent before."

"I'll backtrack. A celebration of the purchase of your very own home. Better?"

"Thank you. Just a coffee. Unless you'd split a muffin with me?"

Luke gave their order. "Two coffees and a blueberry muffin." Charlotte smiled approval and the waitress left.

"How've you been?" Charlotte averted her eyes to look out the window instead of at Luke. She looked back and gently touched his beard roughened cheek where the bruising still showed. Warmth radiated from her. "How did you get that?" She dropped her hand to the table. He wanted her touch back.

"Yeah, that happened the other night. I was jumped from behind in the parking lot of Jim's bar. I screwed up. I let Grant get the jump on me. I should ask you how you've been. I would've called to check on you. You know that, right? I just didn't want to be that guy who's always in your face, not giving you room to breathe."

"I had some time to think. I've made mistakes, too. I'm sorry for running out on you after the fire. I could've called you." Her downcast eyes and stooped shoulders belied the confident woman Luke knew Charlotte Cavanaugh to be. As if she read his mind, she sat straighter and cleared her throat. "Even if after today you only want to remain friends, I would still be the luckiest person." He tried to say something. "Let me finish. Luke, I appreciate that you were there for me and let me have my meltdown in the privacy of your home instead of in a hotel, alone. I also appreciate that you came to check up on me at the office. Your help and comfort helped me more than I can say. The fact that you gave me the space I asked for me means everything."

He smiled at her, feeling like he had already made steps toward mending at least their friendship. "My turn?" She nodded. "My heart dropped when I heard about the fire. There wasn't a place in the world I would have rather been than helping you. As for your friend with the gun, well, he won't be bothering anyone for a while. I know you cared for him once, so I hope he can get counseling or something to help him out. Now that we've cleared that up, can we start over? Friends?"

She reached out and held his hands. "One last thing. Why didn't you tell me that you owned the house?"

"Thinking about it now, it seems silly, but I took it to heart. I made a promise to my mother. When she told me she left the house to me in her will, I made a promise to her that I would either raise my own family there, or I would make sure the person who bought it would treasure the house as much as she did."

"I really don't know what to say. I'm honored that you feel I'm worthy."

Just then the waitress came over and placed their coffee cups on the table along with the muffin, which had a candle in it. They both looked at the candle and then at her.

"It seemed like a celebratory muffin," she said. She lit the candle and walked away.

"Go ahead and make a wish, Charlotte," Luke said. "You have a lot ahead of you."

Charlotte closed her eyes. He silently made a wish, too— for her to want her only place in the world to be with him. She pursed her lips and blew out the candle. He wanted to lean over and kiss her in a way that would make her realize

she never wanted to be too independent. That she would always be willing to have him in her life. He would always
watch over her, so when she needed him he would be there
for her.

"Don't you want to know what I wished for?"

"Isn't that bad luck?"

"I think that's only for birthday wishes." They both
laughed. Charlotte split the muffin in two and used her fingers to pinch off a piece to pop into her mouth.

"Well," Luke said. "I think you should keep your wish a
secret and let me know if it comes true."

"I'll do that."

They fell into a comfortable chitchat about weather delays on construction jobs and new clients wanting remodeling
done in time for the holidays. The waitress came to refill their
coffee cups and take the muffin plate away.

Charlotte reached out and Luke willingly let her hold
his hands again. "Luke, I found out how the fire started. I
feel so bad for the Camden's. Grant started that fire. Mr.
Camden though, he couldn't face telling his wife about
losing his job, so he was trying to cut back on expenses—
my decorating bill being the biggest one. He couldn't tell
me, afraid I'd tell his wife. He devised this whole crazy plan
to scare me off. He is the one that vandalized the house. But
Grant was the one who started the fire. He was so desperate
to get back together. I decided to forgive him because I
think he needs help beyond just time. Thinking about it
now, I should have probably insisted he seek some
counseling. I don't know what the police will do. The
Camden family has their own problems to sort out. I don't

want to add to their issues, so I just told them to call if they ever need me."

***

"When Becker jumped me he ranted about setting the fire. Because of Mr. Camden's lies, you almost died in Becker's fire. It's very generous of you to say you forgive Mr. Camden. I don't know if I could've done the same thing. Is that what you've been doing this week? Trying to figure out what to do about the Camdens?"

"I did work a little, too." She laughed and Luke realized how much he loved hearing that laugh. "I was thinking about you, too," she continued. "Since I was in a reflective mood, I decided to work on how to tell you I messed up. You were so kind to me. I loved being with you, having you hold me and comfort me after the fire. And then I walked away. I don't even know why now. I wish you'd told me about owning the house before now. That had to be a terrible burden to keep. It's very sweet though how you were honoring your mom's wishes. You can trust I will cherish every nook and cranny of that old place. Maybe you can show me some of the more hidden features and not just the dirty, buggy cellar.

"That's a deal I can't pass up."

Luke reached for her hand and gently squeezed. "I have a hidden talent." Charlotte laughed. "Yes, I can see into the future and yours will have all you wish for."

"Really?"

"Charlotte, I'd like to be around to see all that happen."

She was nodding her head in agreement. "I don't want a misunderstanding to get in the way of what's happening with us. At least I think there's an 'us.'"

Luke turned her hands over and ran his thumb along the inside of her wrists. "I'd like to think there was starting to be an 'us,' too. You have a lot of changes going on, so let's take baby steps. Oh, and let's face it. You need me for my truck."

Charlotte gave him a questioning look. "Your truck?"

"You need my muscle to help you move into that big rambling house you just bought."

Chapter Twenty-Four

THREE WEEKS OF homeownership, and Charlotte was very surprised at how well maintained Luke kept the old house. Sure, he is a construction guy, and lots of friends in the trade—but like her new friend Stella said, their own houses were always the last to get worked on.

The new furnace had been installed just the day before, and Charlotte waited for the electrician Luke had recommended to arrive and install the new service for the house and go over any potential issues.

Design books on one side and fiction on the other lined the shelves in the library. Charlotte absorbed the calm of the setting in her executive chair behind the desk, which had only just arrived. New client files sat neatly stacked off to the side awaiting a designated spot. A red breast robin flew past the window completing the serene scene.

Tick, tick, ticking off in the distance caught Charlotte's attention. If she was correct, she was glad she wasn't hearing splash, splash, splashing. The noise wasn't loud, but it was definitely a dripping sound. She got up from her spot and walked around the house to find the offensive noise.

"Oh hell!"

The screen door at the back of the house slammed shut announcing Luke's entrance. She'd given him a key—well, given it back to him. He walked into the kitchen and had the nerve to laugh.

"What the hell are you doing?" he was finally able to spit out. Sam the dog excitedly jumped in the puddle on the floor.

"Don't just stand there. I think the pipe burst under the sink, and I can't get the water to stop." She knew she looked ridiculous. She had on her yoga pants and sleeveless workout top with her Wellington boots.

Luke went to the closet. What was he doing, getting a coat? "Seriously, at a time like this you leave me high and dry?" Charlotte said indignantly.

He walked back into the room. "I have to say, you most definitely don't look dry."

"Smartass. Hey, the water stopped."

"I turned off the main water valve."

"I love you!" She threw herself at him and kissed him hard on the lips.

He wrapped his arms around her and kissed her back.

"I think I should've been hanging around your jobs more often. It's a turn-on watching you fix things."

"Ms. Cavanaugh, I think you're going to make me blush."

"Thank you, Luke. Seriously, not for just turning a knob, but for being my friend." She slid her hands down his chest.

He tilted her head to look up at him. "You're welcome. Can I be selfish now?"

"I think you've earned it."

"Good, because I don't want to be your friend anymore."

He scooped her up. With her arms still around his neck, he held her legs to straddle him. "I love you, too, Charlotte. I don't even know if you realize you told me you love me, but I heard it." He kissed her hard and fast on the lips. "Being with you and feeling like I couldn't show you how I actually felt had been killing me. Your smile and kind heart and brilliance and strong mind make me want to keep you mine forever. My momma would kill me if I didn't court you properly, so I'm asking, Charlotte, would you like to be my girlfriend?"

"God, Luke, I would've loved to have met your mom just to tell her how amazing her son is. I may have said in jest that I love you, but I mean it. Luke Anderson, yes, I would love to go steady."

They both laughed. He put her back on her feet. Charlotte placed her hand on his fuzzy cheek. The gentleness of her touch soothed his racing heart. How could one woman know just what to do?

"Have I mentioned I love when you have a scruffy beard? I also have something to ask." The tick of the clock gave away her nervousness. "Would you fix my broken water pipe?"

This woman knew how to control everything in business. It's what made her successful. Luke understood just how much she had put aside to ask him for help, and he couldn't be more proud of her, love her more for it.

"You know I could do this in no time flat?" She bit her lip and nodded. "You also know that I love that you asked me to help you."

She smiled up at him. "Yes. You are going to help me though, right?"

He kissed her smack dab on the lips. "Babe, I'm going to do you one better. I'm going to show *you* how to fix it."

"Oh man! Now . . . now is the time you decide to not take charge of everything?"

He smacked her on the bottom. "Get a move on little lady. You have plumbing to fix."

My Inspiration

WHILE I WAS too young to go into the woods to see the house in all its glory, there really was a house in the wooded area near where I grew up. To this day, the property is still owned by the Whiting family. The mystery of why a house stood unoccupied in the woods for so long still fascinates me. Unfortunately, once I was old enough to go up to see the house, what I remember is the burned out shell of a magnificent structure and a brick chimney still standing. It was a sight to behold, and the stories that ran through my mind of bygone days were endless. I just wish I had gotten to see it before the fire.

It was only recently that I started a conversation with my real life Charlotte, which got me thinking about that house in the woods again. It was easy to weave my Charlotte into a story about my mysterious house. My Charlotte really is an interior designer who happened to live in a fantastic historic home in Connecticut. She spent many years designing an amazing home for her family, and now enjoys bringing the dreams of her clients to life.

So you see, it was a natural fit to bring Charlotte and the house in the woods together. It took just half an hour to come up with the initial concept. While the story is a work of fiction, it is based on a person whom I cherish and a home that has fascinated me.

HOLYOKE DAILY TRANSCRIPT AND TELEGRAM, FRIDAY, MAY 12, 1939

The Whiting Home On Homestead Avenue

Mr. and Mrs. Fairfield Whiting are living in their new home on Homestead avenue south of the Aeremont highway. Allen Cox, Boston architect and former Holyoker, drew the plans.

White & Wyckoff

Photo given by:
Holyoke Public Library History Room. Holyoke, Massachusetts.

Other Books By
Aly Grady

The Racer's Widow
Chasing the Dream
Taking a Chance

CPSIA information can be obtained
at www.ICGtesting.com
Printed in the USA
LVOW11s0857081017
551660LV00001B/106/P